BRICK GREEK MYTHS

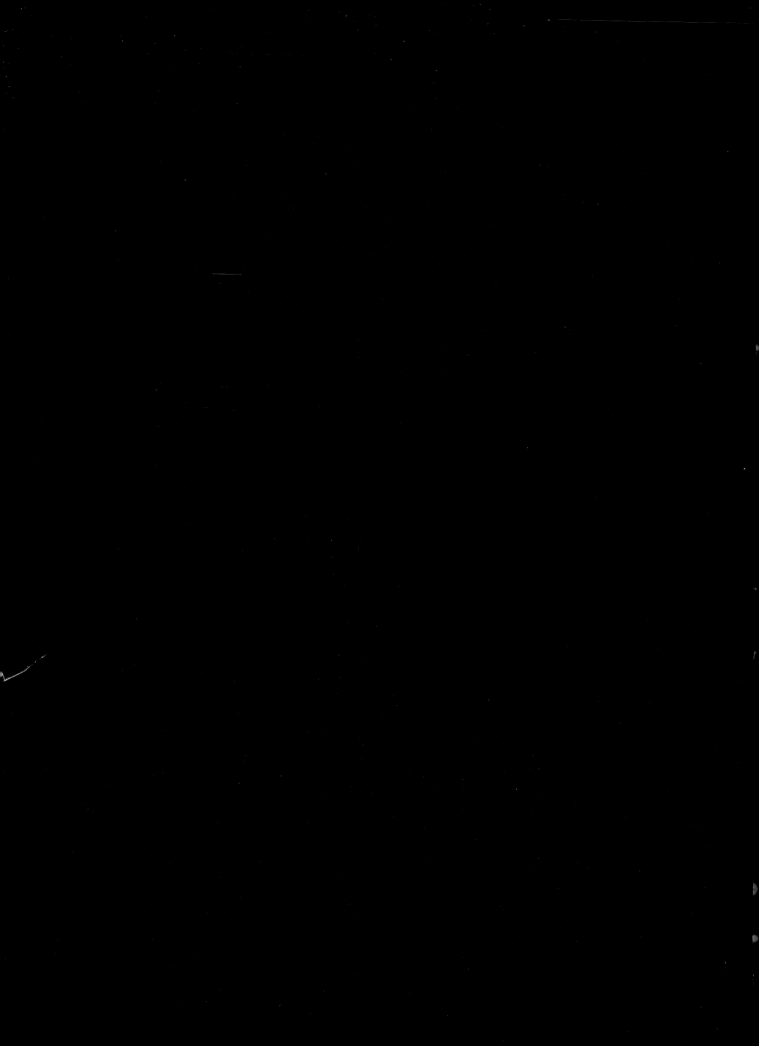

BRICK GREEK MYTHS
THE STORIES OF HERACLES, ATHENA, PANDORA, POSEIDON, AND OTHER ANCIENT HEROES OF MOUNT OLYMPUS

AMANDA BRACK, MONICA SWEENEY,
AND BECKY THOMAS

Skyhorse Publishing

Acknowledgments

This fifth installment of our *Brick* books would not be in print without the amazing people standing behind it. Thank you to our lovely editor Kelsie Besaw, who has continued to shepherd this series to be what it is today. To Tony Lyons, Bill Wolfsthal, and Linda Biagi, for giving us the opportunity to tell so many great stories, and to everyone behind the scenes at Skyhorse for bringing this book to market. Extra special thanks go to Holly Schmidt and Allan Penn for giving us the means build our Brick Empire.

Amanda Brack:

A big thanks to my Mom and Dad for buying us mountains of Legos—who knew it would pay off! More importantly, thank you for your unwavering support and love throughout all my crazy endeavors. Another thanks to my brothers for keeping me away from Barbie dolls, teasing me constantly, and giving me so many wonderful memories. To Andy: thank you for your honesty, for believing in me even when I don't, and for weekly burritos. Last but not least, I must acknowledge my dog, Kemi, because she is the best thing on four legs.

Becky Thomas:

I would like to thank my mom and dad, for reading to me every night and filling me with a love of stories. Thanks to my siblings, Michael, Elizabeth, and Kaitlyn, for keeping things loud and always interesting! Thank you to my husband Patrick for our epic house-wide nerf battles and for his endless support and love. Finally, I want to thank my Professor Marios Philippides for inspiring me in his compelling, fascinating class on Greek mythology.

Monica Sweeney:

Warm hugs go to my incredible sister Katie, who read Greek myths to me when we were little girls and who always encourages my undertakings, big and small. To Sarah Sweeney-Feuerstein, for being Mayor of Legoland. To my Mom, Dad, and Joanne, for being the very best and most supportive parents. To Dr. Anthony Tuck, for teaching an absorbing Greek mythology class and for providing exceptional materials that helped support the research in this book. And a special thank you to Professor Jenny Adams, because I don't know if bawdy Chaucer will make his way to Brick form, but your influence continues to mean so much.

INTRODUCTION BY THE AUTHORS

The stories of Greek mythology have been told and retold since the earliest days of Greek civilization, starting around the mid-sixth century BCE. These myths, like myths across the world, explain how the world came to be and tell the tales of the gods, heroes, and the great figures who shaped it.

Some stories, like *The Iliad*, are based in historical fact and, as such, are more rightly considered sagas than folktales or myths. In these cases, the story began in truth, but years and generations of retelling acted as a game of telephone; the myths and stories we have at this end of history arrive with exaggerations and dramatic flourishes that make each story something quite different from how it started.

Other stories are more like what Rudyard Kipling would call "Just So Stories"; they seek to explain something about the physical world by telling how it came to be. In the realm of mythology, we refer to these as *etiological* narratives. The story of Persephone explains why we have seasons, and the story of Athena and Poseidon's contest for Athens seeks to explain quite a bit about the city's geography and even how it got its name. Each of these stories carries along a *mytheme*, or a basic element that contributes to the formula of the story—whether it is a hero's *katabasis*, or descent to the underworld to fulfill a task, a damsel in distress, or a king's fear of usurpation. These tales, too, are subject to the historical party game and show how our storytelling may change, but our desire to rationalize the origins of all things does not.

Unlike the other stories we have put into brick form, these Greek myths do not have an official text. Of course, the most famous versions of these stories can be found in writing in the works of famous Greek figures, like Hesiod's *The Theogony*, and Homer's *The Iliad* and *The Odyssey*, but even these were passed down as rhapsodies and poems before they were finally written down many years later. Still, these records and other writings are the clearest, most complete tellings of many of the myths, along with clues from contemporary art and pottery and other traditions recounting the myths. This is why there is so much variation in the way that myths are told: without a source, a text to keep the stories honest, they are free to change and bend depending on the whim of the teller. This is our version, and while we did our best to stay true to the stories as we have heard them, we hope we have added a bit of ourselves to the stories, too.

CONTENTS

Dramatis Personae

Aphrodite, goddess of love, beauty, and fertility

Ares, god of war

Artemis, goddess of the hunt, the moon, wilderness, chastity, and archery

Athena, virgin goddess of wisdom, crafts, skill, mathematics, courage, and just warfare

Dionysus, god of wine, ecstasy, theater, and merrymaking

Hephaestus, god of fire, the forge, metalwork, sculpture, and volcanoes

Hera, goddess of women, marriage, and birth

Hermes, messenger of the gods; guide to the Underworld; god of travelers, trade, and athletics

Poseidon, god of the sea, the storm, earthquakes, and horses

Zeus, ruler of Mount Olympus; god of the sky, justice, law and order, lightning, and

Andromeda, beautiful daughter of Cassiopeia

Atlas, titan of astronomy and navigation

Atalanta, the virgin huntress and Arcadian princess

Daedalus, architect of the Labyrinth

Eurydice, oak nymph and daughter of Apo

Hades, god of the underworld, dead, and hidden wealth of the earth

Heracles, divine hero

Jason, heroic leader of the Argonauts

King Eurystheus, king of Tiryns

King Minos, king of Crete

Medusa, gorgon and mother of Pegasus and Chrysaor

The Minotaur, half bull and half man; prisoner of the Labyrinth

Narcissus, hunter plagued by beauty

Orpheus, great musician and poet

Pandora, first human woman

Persephone, Queen of

Perseus, Greek hero

Phaethon, mortal son

Prometheus, titan;

Tantalus, receiver of

Creation and the Birth of Zeus

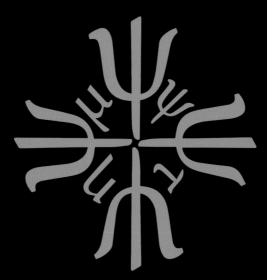

From Chaos came Erebus, or Darkness, and Nyx, or Night.

In the beginning, there was nothing but Chaos: a great chasm of nothingness that stretched across existence.

Eros, or love, came from the chaos and created Aether and Hemera, light and day.

Chaos also bore Mother Earth, called Gaia. Gaia in turn created Ourea and Pontus: the mountains and the sea.

She also created Uranus, god of the heavens.

Gaia and Uranus fell in love and eventually married.

The couple created a family of very strong creatures and deities. Gaia gave birth to the Cyclopes, the three Hecatoncheires,

and the twelve Titans.

But Uranus was a terrible father who did not know how to control his children. He imprisoned the Hecatoncheires in Gaia's womb, buried deeply in the earth.

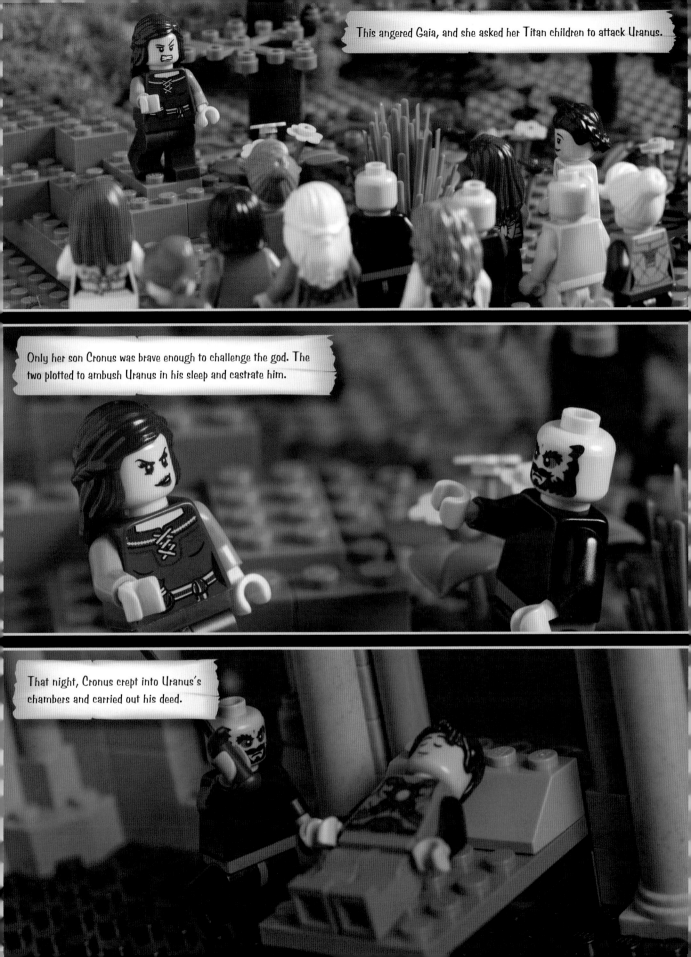

This angered Gaia, and she asked her Titan children to attack Uranus.

Only her son Cronus was brave enough to challenge the god. The two plotted to ambush Uranus in his sleep and castrate him.

That night, Cronus crept into Uranus's chambers and carried out his deed.

Uranus awoke too late to stop Cronus's mutilation, and he fled in pain and anger, promising to have his revenge on Cronus and the rest of the Titans.

His first act was to imprison the Hecatoncheires and the Cyclopes deep underground in Tartarus.

He then took Rhea, a Titan goddess, as his bride.

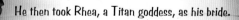

Gaia and Uranus had prophesied that Cronus would be overthrown by one of his children. When Cronus heard this, he devised a plan to hold onto his throne.

Cronus devoured his children, swallowing Hestia, Demeter, Hera, Hades, and Poseidon, one at a time. This way they could not challenge his authority.

Rhea was furious at her husband, so she decided to trick him the next time she was pregnant.

Cronus was fooled and swallowed the stone, satisfied that his throne was still secure.

The next time that she bore a child, she gave the baby to the nymphs to care for. Then she went to Cronus to present his latest child to him, replacing the baby with a stone.

The baby she saved was called Zeus. He was raised on the island of Crete and grew to be smart and strong.

Zeus wanted to find a way to save his siblings from his father's stomach, so he went to speak with Metis, a Titan of great wisdom.

She created a potion that would make Cronus sick and empty his stomach, and she gave it to Zeus.

Rhea then convinced Cronus to allow young Zeus to act as his cupbearer on Mount Olympus.

Zeus covertly added the potion to his father's drink, acting so quickly that no one saw him. Then he gave the drink to Cronus, who drank it down.

As soon as he had finished the drink, Cronus began to vomit violently, and Zeus's siblings emerged unscathed from their father's stomach.

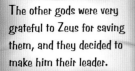

The other gods were very grateful to Zeus for saving them, and they decided to make him their leader.

But Cronus still had no desire to give up his throne to his son. Though the young deities were instantly full-grown, he still refused to let them take their rightful places as gods.

The rest of the Titans also resisted the new generation: this conflict soon came to a head in the great battle called the Titanomachy, in which the new gods fought the Titans for control over the earth.

This war went on for ten years without a victory on either side.

While the Titans fought from Mount Othrys, Zeus and his siblings set themselves up on Mount Olympus.

As the war raged on, Zeus decided to call in some allies. He went to Tartarus and freed the Hecatoncheires and the Cyclopes from their chains.

Before they could fight, the monsters first needed to be fed.

So Zeus brought them ambrosia, the nectar of the gods, and fed them. They were refreshed and invigorated and agreed to join Zeus in his battle.

In gratitude for freeing them, the Cyclopes gave Zeus the power to create thunder and lightning.

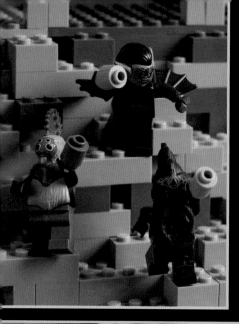

As the battle began, the Hecatoncheires threw heavy rocks at the Titans at impossible speeds.

At the height of the conflict, Zeus instructed his siblings to flee up the mountain, drawing the Titans into a trap.

The Titans fell for Zeus's trick and followed the Olympians into the ambush.

Once the Titans were in range, the Olympians and their allies attacked.

The Titans were overwhelmed by the onslaught, and Zeus soon claimed victory.

He bound the Titans in chains and sent them to Tartarus.

There they were guarded by the Hecatoncheires to keep them from escaping.

Gaia had not gotten involved in the great battle, but when she saw that her children the Titans had been imprisoned, she was very angry.

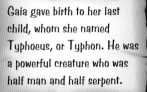

Gaia gave birth to her last child, whom she named Typhoeus, or Typhon. He was a powerful creature who was half man and half serpent.

All of the Olympians except Zeus fled from the creature. They ran to Egypt, where they disguised themselves as animals.

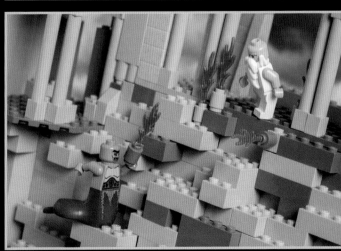

Typhoeus went to Mount Olympus and attacked the home of the gods, spitting great flaming stones and hot fire from his mouth.

Zeus battled hard against the creature with his powerful lightning bolts.

At last he struck Typhoeus, gravely injuring him.

Seeing his foe was weak, Zeus challenged him to hand-to-hand combat.

Typhoeus wrapped his coils around the god and squeezed him tight. Then he took a knife and cut Zeus's tendons, leaving him helpless.

He brought Zeus to a cave and imprisoned him there.

Zeus's son Hermes came to save him. He snuck into the cave and fixed Zeus's tendons.

Zeus healed quickly, and escaped the cave, returning to attack Typhoeus from his chariot.

He fought hard against the monster, flinging sizzling bolts of lightning in quick succession.

Finally, he slayed the terrible creature.

He buried the body beneath Mount Etna, and the great mountain has belched smoke and ash ever since.

The last foes Zeus had to face were the giants.

The giants were also the children of Gaia and Uranus.

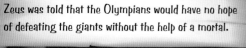
Zeus was told that the Olympians would have no hope of defeating the giants without the help of a mortal.

Clever Gaia overheard this prophecy and began to search for an herb that would protect her children from mortal hands.

Zeus saw her plan, and he cloaked the earth in darkness to keep her from finding what she sought, then he took the herbs himself.

Then he summoned the half-mortal hero Heracles to help them fight.

Iris, the messenger god, called together all of the gods in Olympus to discuss the war.

Gaia freed the giants and sent them after Zeus and the other gods, since they had banished her elder children, the Titans, to Tartarus.

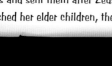

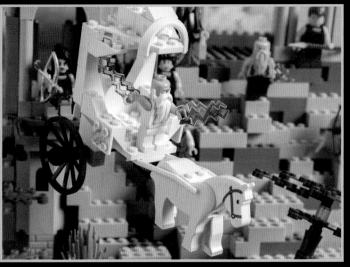

The great battle soon began, right at the foot of Mount Olympus. Zeus threw his terrible lightning bolts, sending fire raining through the air.

Gaia set her feet against the ground and created violent earthquakes.

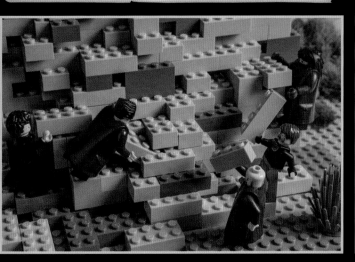

The giants leveled mountains, tearing rocks and boulders from the cliffs and sending them flying.

The giants then took up rocks and trees to throw at Mount Olympus.

During the fray, Ares killed the giant Pelorus from his war chariot.

Then Heracles shot the giant Alcyoneus. But because he was still connected to Gaia, his mother, he did not die.

So Heracles went and picked Alcyoneus up over his head so that he could not touch the ground. Separated from the life-power of his mother, the giant died.

Heracles and Zeus finished off another giant named Porphyrion by striking him with an arrow and a lightning bolt at once.

The giant Ephialtes was killed by Apollo and Heracles, who shot arrows into the creature's eyes.

The rest of the gods helped to finish off the giants that were left.

When the battle was over, the new gods had won. Zeus thanked them all, and named them Olympians.

The gods chose Zeus to be their new king and ruler. Zeus happily accepted and began the task of dividing up the domains of the earth and assigning them to the gods.

He took the sky as his own domain.

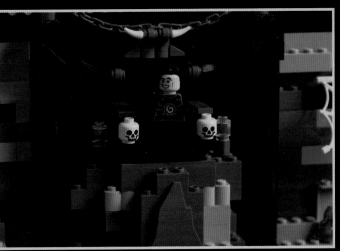

He set up his brother Hades as ruler of the Underworld, and made him the god of the dead and riches of the earth.

Poseidon was given the seas to rule. Zeus handed out assignments to the rest of the gods this way and declared that both Mount Olympus and the earth would be neutral areas.

With those issues solved, Zeus settled down and got married. His wife was Metis, the Titan woman who had helped him poison Cronus.

His grandparents, Gaia and Uranus, told Zeus that Metis was destined to bear a very powerful child who would overthrow his father.

Improving on his father's example, Zeus decided to solve this problem by swallowing Metis before she gave birth. When he devoured her, he absorbed her great wisdom and good counsel.

Soon Zeus was plagued by a terrible headache that pained him greatly.

Suddenly his daughter Athena sprung out of his head fully grown and shouting a war cry; she was to be the goddess of war.

Zeus then married his second wife, named Themis, which means steadfast or firm. She was another Titaness and was connected to the ways of the earth, like her mother Gaia. She was also known as the goddess of justice and righteousness.

Their union created prosperity and order, and their combined focus on justice helped them to establish the new government that Zeus had created.

Themis bore Zeus two sets of triplets. The first were the Horae, or the Hours, who represented the seasons of the year. They were connected to fertility and growth.

The second set of triplets were the Moerae, or the Fates. They were Clotho, who spun the thread of fate, Lachesis, who assigned man his fate, and Atropos, the fate that cannot be changed or avoided, also known as the one who cuts the thread at the end of a man's life.

Now that the world was put in order, Zeus decided that they needed joy to put everything in balance.

So he made love to an Oceanid named Eurynome and created the Charities, also known as the Graces. These became the goddesses of festivity and happiness.

Like their sisters the Hours, the Graces were well loved by the gods and were always invited to their feasts.

Then Zeus took Demeter as his fourth wife.

She gave birth to beautiful Persephone, who would come to be the Queen of the Underworld.

Zeus's fifth wife was another Titaness, named Mnemosyne. After Zeus visited her bed nine nights in a row, she bore him nine daughters who were called the Muses.

The Muses created the arts and all other intellectual pursuits and inspired poets and singers and dancers in their art. They were named Clio, Euterpe, Thalia, Melpomene, Terpsichore, Erato, Polyhymnia, Urania, and Calliope.

Later Zeus married his sixth wife, Leto.

She gave birth to the twins Artemis (goddess of the hunt, wild animals, and maidens) and Apollo (god of art and learning).

Zeus's seventh and final wife was the goddess Hera.

She bore Zeus Hebe, the cupbearer for the gods,

Ares, the god of war,

and Eileithyia, who was a goddess of childbirth.

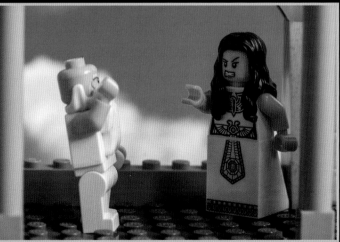

The couple was well-known for their domestic disputes, and Hera had a very hot temper. There was no love between them.

And this is how the gods, the world, and everything in it were created.

Prometheus's Fire and Pandora's Box

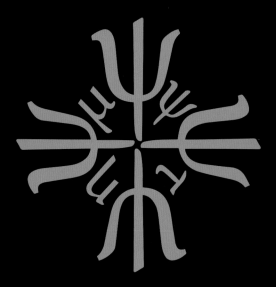

In the beginning of time, the immortal gods and deities of Mount Olympus were all-powerful and prosperous. Mankind was still young and struggled to survive. When the gods drank nectar, people drank from streams. When the gods ate ambrosia, mortals scavenged for food. When Zeus threw his lightning bolts across the sky, men cowered in fear.

Atop Mount Olympus, there was a humble and thoughtful Titan named Prometheus, who was the grandson of Mother Earth, Gaia, and whose name meant "forethought." Growing tired of living idly amongst the other immortals, Prometheus came up with an idea.

He ventured down from the high peaks of Mount Olympus and down to earth to be among the mortals.

Prometheus was shocked and saddened to see how the mortals lived. They had no tools and could not build.

They had no culture and could not make art or find enjoyment. They had no fire, so they ate barbarically and were no better off than the beasts around them.

Prometheus returned to Mount Olympus and asked the omnipotent Zeus for help. If Zeus could just give men the power of fire, then they would be able to cook their food, ward off disease, and protect themselves from danger.

Zeus listened to Prometheus's idea and immediately struck it down. He said that if men were to have fire, then they would grow strong and powerful. So powerful, perhaps, that mortals could one day overthrow the immortals and drive them out of their kingdom atop Mount Olympus.

Frustrated with Zeus's decision, Prometheus ignored his wishes and went to seek the source of fire so he could give it to mankind. He traveled long and far and finally came to a high mountain where the sun met the earth.

Clutching a strand of fennel, Prometheus captured fire from the sun and wielded it on the branch.

Prometheus brought the fire to the mortal men so that they could prosper.

He went on to teach them how to cultivate crops and grow food, how to write and do math so that they could build their culture, and medicinal practices so they could treat the terrible diseases that they had struggled with.

Learning from Prometheus, the men began to thrive. They began to cook their own food, build shelter, farm, and keep animals. They even began to write literature and produce art for entertainment. Seeing what Prometheus had done, Zeus went into a fury. But instead of lashing out and unleashing fiery misery unto the mortals and destroying Prometheus, he cleverly plotted revenge against his misbehaving Titan.

Zeus summoned the other gods of Mount Olympus to take part in his plan, though he did not tell them why. Being the most powerful of all of the divinities, the other gods reluctantly agreed to help. Zeus told them to work together to create the first woman, who would be made in the image of a goddess. The gods began their task, each giving a special gift of theirs to the new and lovely being.

With the help of the Four Winds, Hephaestus, the smith god from far beneath the earth, gathered rich earth and water to begin shaping his gift. He artfully molded clay into the figure of a woman.

Athena, the goddess of many things, including wisdom and skill, taught the woman how to weave and how to make useful and beautiful crafts.

Aphrodite, the goddess of love, was next to contribute, and she offered the woman beauty and charm.

Hermes, the messenger of the gods, offered the woman curiosity.

While the gods worked in secret to make the woman, Prometheus considered what he had done. With the gift of thinking ahead, Prometheus sought out his brother, Epimetheus, whose name meant "afterthought." Prometheus warned his brother that Zeus may try and find a sneaky way to cause them trouble, so he told Epimetheus never to accept gifts from the mighty Zeus.

Back on Mount Olympus, the first woman was complete. The gods name her Pandora, which meant "the all-gifted," for the many precious things that they had given her. Hermes led Pandora down to earth. Playing matchmaker at the request of Zeus, Hermes introduced Pandora and Epimetheus.

In awe of the lovely and beautiful woman, Epimetheus forgot his brother's warning to not trust Zeus. He fell head over heels for Pandora and intended to marry her.

The less powerful divinities were not the only ones to give Pandora a gift. Zeus offered her one as well, presenting her with a golden jar that he said held the most precious of all the things on earth.

Athena, in her great wisdom, warned Pandora that she should never open the gift.

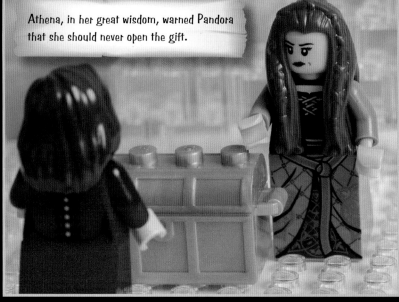

She explained that the golden box contained the gifts of life and death and other precious things that Zeus did not have the authority to give. Only Gaia, mother of the earth, had the power to give these things away.

Cursed with curiosity, Pandora became more and more drawn to the contents of the box.

Pandora marveled at the box and wondered if perhaps it contained precious jewels. Knowing that gems and jewelry could only add to her beauty, she pondered ways to sneak a peek. Epimetheus, not realizing how overwhelmed his wife was with curiosity, left Pandora by herself with the golden box.

Pandora's new husband, Epimetheus, now realizing that the gift may be a part of Zeus's wrathful nature, warned her not to open the box.

The intrigue was just too much for her, and despite all the warnings she had received, Pandora decided to open the box.

The lid had barely creaked apart when a gust of wind burst the box open. Out sprung the world's darkest creatures, which unleashed infinite forms of human suffering that had never before been experienced by the mortals or the gods alike.

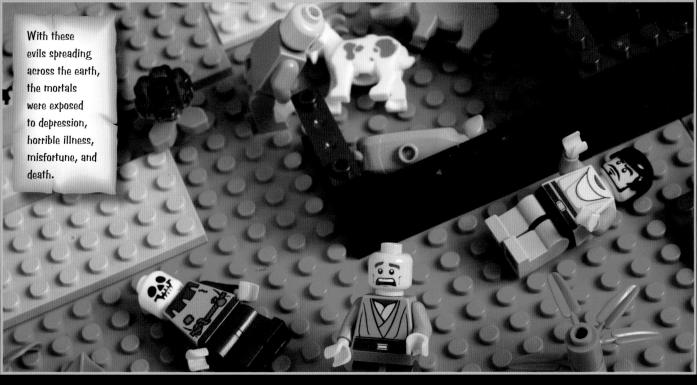

With these evils spreading across the earth, the mortals were exposed to depression, horrible illness, misfortune, and death.

As the evil rushed out of the box, Pandora tried her hardest to snap it shut. Though she succeeded, all of the world's darkest creatures had been released. Yet one thing remained: hope. With hope protected inside the box, humanity would still have a fighting chance against the disaster forced upon them.

From high atop Mount Olympus, Zeus watched as Prometheus's hard work in helping humanity unraveled. While they still had hope, life on earth would soon be much trickier for the mortals.

Phaethon and the Chariot of the Sun

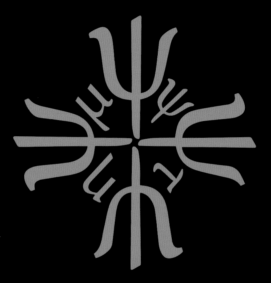

Young Phaethon, whose name meant "the radiant one," was the half-mortal son of Phoebus Apollo, god of the sun. One day he decided to pay his father a visit.

He came to Phoebus Apollo as he sat on his throne, cloaked in crimson and surrounded by the seasons.

The sun god asked Phaethon what business he wished to discuss.

Phaethon complained that mankind had been mocking him, claiming that he was not really the son of a god.

He asked his father to help him prove he was the son of a god and begged Phoebus Apollo to give him some token to show his parentage.

Phoebus Apollo embraced his son and promised to help him. He vowed that he would do anything Phaethon asked to prove that he was his father.

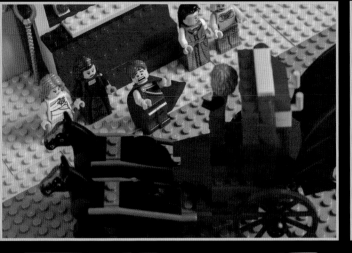

Thrilled, Phaethon asked that he be allowed to drive his father's great winged chariot across the sky for him, only for one day.

The sun god begged him to reconsider, because he was a mortal and the chariot was made for gods to ride.

Phoebus explained that only he could withstand the great heat well enough to guide the chariot where it needed to go.

But Phaethon would not listen and pleaded with his father for the chariot.

Phoebus relented, as he could not go back on his word. He put a magic ointment onto Phaethon's face to protect him from the chariot's heat.

He instructed Phaethon not to go near the north or south poles, and to drive slowly, being careful not to let the chariot go too low, lest it burn the earth, or too high, lest it scorch the sky.

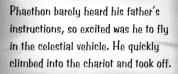

Phaethon barely heard his father's instructions, so excited was he to fly in the celestial vehicle. He quickly climbed into the chariot and took off.

He had not flown far before he began having trouble controlling the horses. They bucked and reared under his inexperienced hand, flying erratically.

They flew higher and higher into the heavens, and Phaethon began to panic as he found himself surrounded by stars.

Then the chariot plunged, bringing them closer and closer to the earth. The land began to smoke and flame.

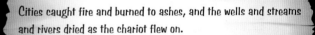

Cities caught fire and burned to ashes, and the wells and streams and rivers dried as the chariot flew on.

Soon the chariot burned so hot that Phaethon himself caught fire.

He toppled from the chariot and fell straight into the river Eridanus below.

When he landed in the river, the water closed over his head and he was gone.

His father watched the scene from his throne, helpless to intervene to save his son or stop the fiery destruction.

It is said that day brought no light to the world.

Hades, Persephone, and the Story of the Seasons

Persephone was born as the daughter of Demeter, goddess of the harvest, and Zeus, king of the gods.

She spent an idyllic childhood on Mount Olympus, playing games and sharing secrets with her half sisters Athena and Aphrodite.

As she got older, she became more and more beautiful. It became clear she was going to be a woman of rare and renowned beauty.

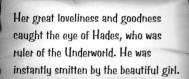

Her great loveliness and goodness caught the eye of Hades, who was ruler of the Underworld. He was instantly smitten by the beautiful girl.

Hades went to Zeus and asked for his permission to marry Persephone. Zeus accepted Hades's proposal but did not tell Persephone or her mother.

Soon after, Persephone went for a walk through the rolling hills to pick flowers. She walked happily, singing as she stooped to gather the lovely blooms.

Suddenly, the ground split and a great crevasse opened in the earth.

From the crevasse sprang Hades, riding his chariot. When Persephone realized what was happening, she began to scream! Hades scooped her up and put her in his chariot, and together they went down the crevasse to the Underworld.

Once there, Hades told her that she was to be his queen.

Persephone soon came to love Hades and her new role as Queen of the Underworld.

Still, she missed her mother and the world above.

Demeter, unaware of her daughter's fate, searched across the face of the earth for Persephone.

She finally came to the town of Eleusis and set herself down by the great fountain there.

Stripped of her vitality and wilted from her hopeless search for her daughter, Demeter looked old and wrinkled.

Four young women came upon Demeter and decided to bring her home with them.

The sisters brought Demeter to their parents, who welcomed her warmly. They offered her a place to stay, and hired her to care for their young son.

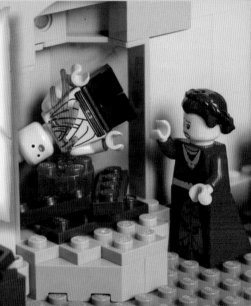

One morning the child's mother was awakened before Demeter, and seeing her child in the fire, was filled with fear for him.

As a gift to the family, Demeter decided to make the young boy immortal. To do so, she placed him in the fire each night and then took him out in the morning.

The horrorstruck family angrily demanded that Demeter leave their home.

Demeter's passion was enflamed, and suddenly she was transformed into her true form.

The family, realizing her identity, begged for her forgiveness and vowed to build a temple in her honor, where they would teach the secrets of immortality.

Still, she left them and continued with her search. She met with Hecate, goddess of witchcraft, who said she had heard Persephone calling out the day she disappeared. Hecate suggested that Demeter talk to Helios, the sun god, to ask if he saw what had happened that day.

Demeter went to Helios to question him.

He told her how Persephone was taken away by Hades, and how Zeus had given his permission for the match.

Demeter went to Zeus to ask him to intervene and bring her daughter back to her.

When he refused, Demeter was filled with rage and vowed to withhold her blessing from the earth until the day she was reunited with Persephone.

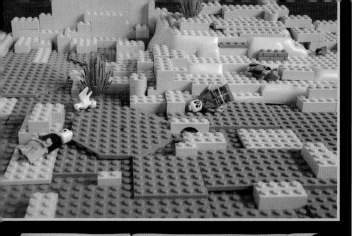

As the goddess of the harvest withdrew her spiritual blessings, crops stopped growing and plants withered in the field. The land was struck with famine, and many people starved and died.

Seeing the destruction Demeter had caused, Zeus relented and sent Hermes to bring Persephone back from the Underworld.

Persephone still missed her mother, but in this time apart, she had grown quite fond of her husband Hades and her role as Queen of the Underworld.

She was a very good and kind queen, and she took her responsibilities seriously.

And so, before she was to leave, Hades offered her a pomegranate to eat.

Persephone knew that if she were to eat in the Underworld, she would not be allowed to leave, so she opened the fruit and ate seven of the tart little seeds inside.

Now Persephone was bound to the Underworld. But clever Hermes soon came up with a compromise.

Since she had only eaten a small portion of the pomegranate, she would be allowed to return to the surface for most of the year. When she was with Demeter, the goddess of the harvest was joyful and content, and the earth was warm and fertile.

But for four months of the year, Persephone rejoined her husband in the Underworld and again took up her responsibilities as queen.

Demeter mourned the loss of her daughter again each year. Now, as the months grow closer to Persephone's absence, Demeter grows wary and the leaves begin to fall, signaling autumn. And for those four months when Persephone lives in the Underworld, the earth is barren and cold, and nothing grows. We call this season winter.

But when winter is over, and Persephone visits her mother, we celebrate spring, as the world blooms with joy that the goddess's daughter has returned.

Eurydice and Orpheus

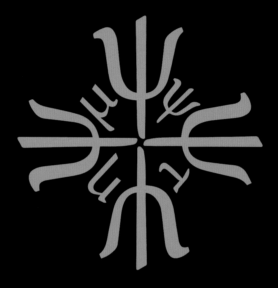

Once there was a very talented young man named Orpheus. He was the son of Apollo, god of the stringed instrument, and he was gifted with great musical skill.

He was so talented that when he played his lute and sang, no mortal could resist his song. Even the animals and rocks and trees were drawn to his music.

One day as he was playing, a beautiful wood nymph named Eurydice sat down beside him to listen.

She was bewitched by his song, and he by her beauty, and as she listened they both fell deeply in love with one another.

They decided right away that they should be married.

The very next day, they came together under the trees, and Hymenaios, the god of marriage himself, blessed their union.

Then they celebrated with a huge feast that lasted all day. There was plenty of food and wine and many friends to join in their joy.

But not everyone was happy. As they celebrated, a man named Aristaeus looked on angrily. He was a local shepherd who desired beautiful Eurydice and hated Orpheus. As the new couple feasted, he plotted a way to separate them.

He decided that he would kill Orpheus so he could steal Eurydice away.

After the celebration, the couple went for a walk through the woods together.

Aristaeus slunk along close behind them, armed and ready to carry out his plan.

The lovers spied him just in time and fled in a panic, narrowly avoiding the shepherd's attack.

But still he continued to pursue them, chasing them through fields and forests, on and on until they were exhausted.

Eurydice tripped and stumbled over her weary feet, until, trailing behind Orpheus, she fell to the ground.

He turned to help her to her feet,

but to his horror he found that she had fallen right into a nest of snakes and had been bitten by one of the poisonous creatures.

Aristaeus realized she was dying and gave up his chase.

Orpheus had no way to save his love, but he wept and embraced her as she died in his arms.

Lost and alone, Orpheus was consumed with grief. He decided to seek his bride in the Underworld and bring her back. Armed with his lute, Orpheus passed through a cave to the gates of the Underworld.

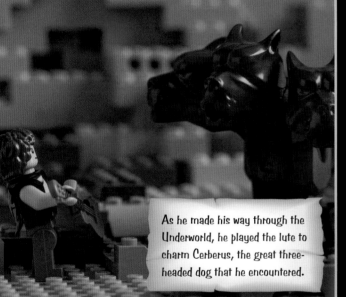

As he made his way through the Underworld, he played the lute to charm Cerberus, the great three-headed dog that he encountered.

In this way he passed through the dangerous lands of the dead safely.

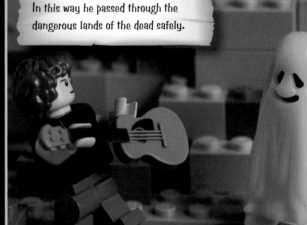

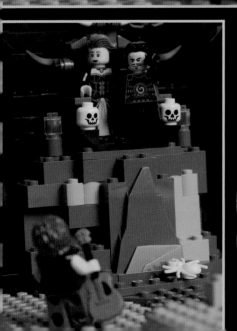

Finally he reached the throne of the Underworld, where Hades and his queen, Persephone sat in state.

He played beautiful music for the couple, picking out the most lovely, mournful songs he could think of.

Hades declared that they would let Eurydice follow him out of the Underworld.

The beautiful songs reminded Hades of how he had fallen in love with his own bride, and he was greatly troubled by the thought of being separated from his cherished Persephone. The god and queen of the Underworld were touched by Orpheus's music, and they decided to help him.

But Orpheus must abide by one rule: he could not turn to look at his love until they had made it safely out of the cave and into the light of day. If he looked on her, she must return to the Underworld forever.

So Orpheus set out for the surface, with Eurydice following behind him. They traveled back through the dangerous lands Orpheus had explored before, and he kept his lute ready in case of trouble.

At last they reached the door of the cave, and Orpheus rejoiced to feel the warm sun on his face.

He happily turned to embrace his beloved Eurydice and rejoice at their reunion. But she was still in darkness, and as Orpheus set his eyes on her, she disappeared back into the void.

Orpheus was seized with overwhelming despair.

He tried to follow her into the Underworld again, but Charon, the ferryman for the river Styx, would not let him through.

Heartsick, Orpheus wandered the earth, sad and hopeless.

Now his songs were sad, though they were still as beautiful as ever.

Many women fell in love with him for his beautiful music, but he would love no one other than Eurydice.

One group of women was particularly angry that he had rejected them, and they went to confront Orpheus.

They attacked him, throwing sharp sticks and heavy rocks.

But Orpheus played his music, and the rocks and sticks were so enchanted they refused to strike him.

Frustrated and furious, the women tore Orpheus to pieces, pulling him limb from limb.

They threw his body and his lute into the river and left him.

Orpheus floated in pieces down the river until he reached the island where the muses lived.

The muses pulled him from the river and gave him a proper burial, putting his lute over his grave to mark the place.

Once buried, Orpheus was able to return to the Underworld, where at long last he was reunited with his beloved Eurydice.

Athena and Poseidon's Contest for Athens

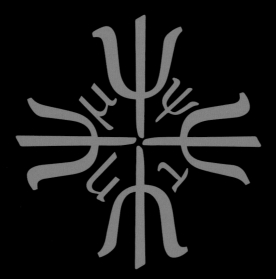

Once, far in the past of Athens's history, the city was ruled by a king named Cecrops.

At this time, Athens had no patron deity, so King Cecrops set out to find one.

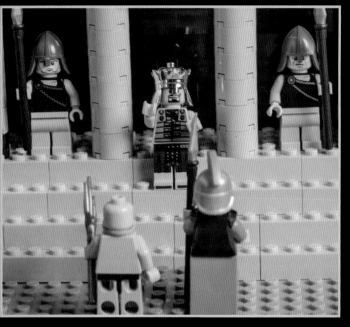

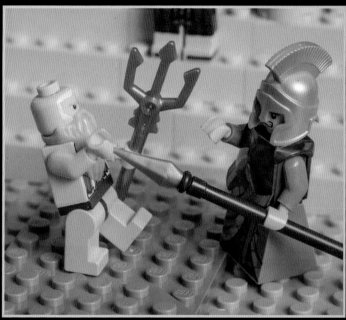

The king spoke to the gods Poseidon and Athena, who both wished to be the patron of the prosperous city.

The rivalry was fierce, with both gods determined to call Athens their own. The fight became so intense that it almost started a war.

The people of the city did not want to have to choose between the two gods, because they feared they would be punished by whoever lost.

Athena suggested that they solve the problem by holding a contest between the two deities.

She proposed that they both choose a gift to give the people of Athens. Whoever could give the best gift would be the official deity of the city.

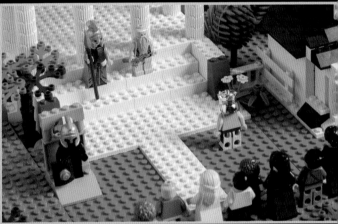

King Cecrops would be the judge of the gifts and decide which god was victorious.

When it was time to present their gifts, the gods went up to the Acropolis, the huge ancient fortress that still sits on the rocky cliffs high above the city.

Poseidon presented his gift first. He lifted his trident and struck the earth. A spring called the Erekhtheis instantly burst from the spot where the trident had touched.

The people of Athens were delighted: a spring would help them keep their crops irrigated and growing strong despite the stony Greek soil. However when they realized the spring was salt water, they were dismayed, because it would be of no use to them.

Then it was Athena's turn to present her gift. She showed the Athenians an olive seed.

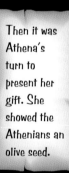

She planted it, and the seed grew into a big strong olive tree. At first the Athenians did not know why she had given them such a humble plant as their gift.

Then Athena explained that olives were useful not only to eat, but for their oil, which was used for lamps, cooking, and as a way to stay clean.

Athena was declared the winner, and her gift of the olive tree is still connected to the city that bears her name.

Poseidon was a sore loser and did not like this outcome. Just as the Athenians suspected, he decided to punish them for rejecting him, so he called the sea to him and flooded the lands around the city, and they remain flooded to this day.

Arachne's Web

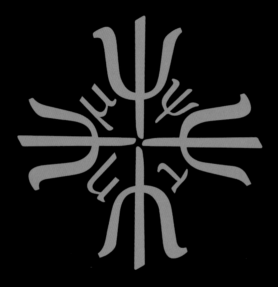

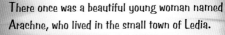
There once was a beautiful young woman named Arachne, who lived in the small town of Ledia.

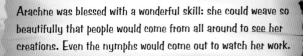
Arachne was blessed with a wonderful skill: she could weave so beautifully that people would come from all around to see her creations. Even the nymphs would come out to watch her work.

Her visitors were amazed with her intricate work, and many would ask if she had learned her craft from Athena, the goddess of weaving and wisdom herself.

Arachne, cursed with vanity, scoffed at the question. It annoyed her that her fans would think her less talented than anyone, even a goddess. She proudly declared that she could weave even better than Athena herself.

Athena, listening nearby, was furious to overhear Arachne's boast. Still, she decided to give the prideful girl a second chance to atone for her great offense.

Athena disguised herself as an old woman and made a visit to Arachne. She advised the young woman to take back her boast and warned her not to offend the gods.

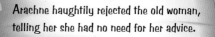
Arachne haughtily rejected the old woman, telling her she had no need for her advice.

She boldly continued that she would welcome a contest of skill with the goddess Athena, and if she were to lose she would take the punishment.

At that moment, Athena threw off her disguise and revealed who she really was. Arachne was aghast at seeing the goddess before her but remained stubborn and refused to bow to her.

Athena, taking Arachne at her word, challenged the young weaver to a direct contest of skill.

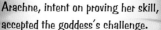
Arachne, intent on proving her skill, accepted the goddess's challenge.

Athena began weaving a tapestry depicting her contest fighting against Poseidon to be the goddess of Athens.

Arachne, meanwhile, created a tapestry criticizing the gods, showing scenes of them tricking and abusing mortals and depicting their worst traits and weaknesses.

When the tapestries were finished and removed from the loom, even Athena was forced to admit that Arachne's work was higher quality than her own.

Enraged by the outcome of the contest and by Arachne's open ridicule of the gods, Athena tore Arachne's tapestry to shreds and pulled her loom to pieces.

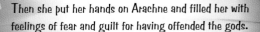

Then she put her hands on Arachne and filled her with feelings of fear and guilt for having offended the gods.

Arachne was filled with grief.

Overwhelmed with the emotions, she quietly died of heartbreak.

Athena regretted driving the young woman to her death.

She decided to bring Arachne back to life, but not as a human. She sprinkled Hecate's potion over Arachne's body,

and transformed the girl into a spider, cursing the girl and her descedents to weave and spin forever.

Perseus's Quest

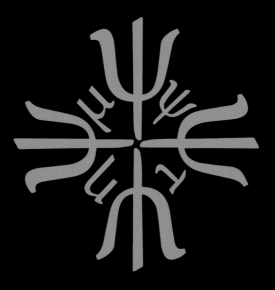

There was once a king named Acrisius who had a beautiful daughter named Danae.

Acrisius spoke to an oracle, who told him that Danae's son would one day overthrow him as ruler.

Fearful that his throne would be usurped, Acrisius locked Danae in a high tower so that she could never marry and have children. The tower was without doors and offered only one window for Danae to look out onto the earth.

One day, as she was sitting in her tower, a golden light suddenly shined into the window, and Zeus appeared before her.

Zeus told Danae how much he admired her. He offered her gifts and beautiful flowers to make her tower less gloomy, and he requested that she marry him.

Beneath the tower, Acrisius noticed the light coming from Danae's window and became suspicious. He tore down the tower walls to reach her.

When he arrived at the top of the tower, he found Danae holding a newborn baby boy in her arms, whom she named Perseus. She looked cheerful and was surrounded by the flowers Zeus had given her.

Acrisius was infuriated. For fear of the prophecy being fulfilled, he locked Danae and baby Perseus in a chest and cast them out to sea.

Zeus witnessed this and guided the chest to safety on the island of Seriphus.

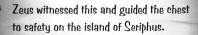

Just offshore, King Polydectes's brother, Dictys, sat in his boat fishing. He saw the chest floating and caught it in his net.

He discovered the mother and child and brought them back to shore.

Both Dictys and Polydectes took care of Danae and Perseus over the next several years.

They raised Perseus to be brave, strong, and noble.

Over time, Polydectes fell in love with Danae and asked her to marry him.

Danae was not interested in marrying him and said no. Enraged at this rejection, Polydectes tried to force Danae into the marriage.

Perseus saw Polydectes attack his mother and immediately intervened. He stood by her to make sure she was not forced into a marriage she did not want.

Feeling rejected and humiliated at Danaë's refusal, Polydectes thought carefully about how to seek his revenge.

He came up with a clever plan and announced that he would marry the daughter of one of his friends.

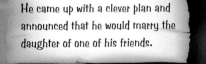

He invited everyone to the wedding and asked that they all bring gifts.

As the wedding commenced, Perseus watched all the guests bring gifts to Polydectes and his new bride. Not having any money, he could not offer a wedding gift to the couple.

Perseus addressed Polydectes and his new wife and announced that, instead of buying them a gift, he would win anything they desired on their behalf.

His plan unfolding just as he had suspected, Polydectes told Perseus which gift he wanted, and it was the most perilous gift of all. He sent Perseus on a dangerous quest for the head of Medusa.

Perseus and Medusa

There once lived a beautiful mortal named Medusa whose name meant "protectress." She was known for her long and lovely flowing hair.

Medusa had two sisters, Sthenno and Euryale, who did not share her beautiful features. They were hideous gorgons, and unlike Medusa, they were immortal.

Medusa was a devoted and innocent priestess of Athena. She was committed to serve Athena for the rest of her life and to never marry.

One day, Medusa caught the attention of Poseidon, the god of the sea.

He approached her, finding her irresistible. Devoted to keeping her vows to Athena, Medusa brushed Poseidon off.

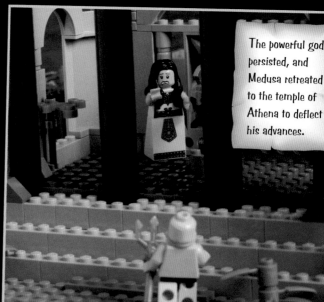

The powerful god persisted, and Medusa retreated to the temple of Athena to deflect his advances.

Poseidon followed her to the temple and, in continuing his attempts to woo her, embraced her.

Athena, knowing the goings-on of her temple, became outraged that Medusa had violated her vows as a priestess, especially in such a sacred place.

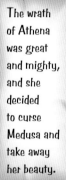

The wrath of Athena was great and mighty, and she decided to curse Medusa and take away her beauty.

She turned Medusa's lovely flowing hair into a mane of slithering, venomous snakes. Medusa became as ugly as her gorgon sisters, and from then on, anyone who dared look on her face was turned to stone.

Medusa looked upon her visage in horror; she was a monster, and her serpent locks made her all the more terrifying. She fled her home, devastated and terrified of hurting those she loved.

In her travels, Medusa's dreadful appearance caused her great misery. Everywhere she went, fearful townspeople clamored for their weapons to ward her off or shunned her if she asked for help. The more Medusa was spurned, the more embittered she became.

As time passed, Medusa slowly became the monster she appeared to be. Many tried to kill her, but the power of her deathly stare was indefensible. Heavily armed brutes and even the most skilled warriors were all frozen in their tracks, perfectly preserved as stone sculptures of their previous forms.

Medusa returned to the lair where her sisters resided and surrounded herself with the statues of the ill-fated foes who dared face her.

Around the same time, the hero Perseus had begun the quest given to him by King Polydectes.

Many of the gods wished Medusa dead, so they armed Perseus with many powerful tools and weapons that could help him defeat her.

The smith god Hephaestus forged him a mighty sword.

Hades, the god of the Underworld, fashioned a helmet of invisibility to help him move stealthily.

And Hermes, the messenger of the gods, gave him gold-winged sandals to help him move with greater swiftness.

Athena, whose curse had brought on Medusa's powers of destruction, provided Perseus with a great mirrored shield.

Perseus stormed Medusa's lair, armed with his gifts from the gods.

He confronted the angry gorgon sorceress, whose serpents hissed and whose ferocious gaze threatened to kill him.

Remembering the shield given to him by Athena, Perseus had an even greater weapon than Medusa's horrific glare.

He protected himself behind his mirror shield, only looking at Medusa through the shield's reflection.

With that, he delivered a powerful swing of his sword and cut off Medusa's monstrous head.

But Medusa had been carrying Poseidon's child, and from out of her neck sprang Pegasus, a vast flying horse.

Then, using his winged shoes and invisibility helmet, Perseus evaded Medusa's sisters and escaped the lair.

Perseus and Atlas

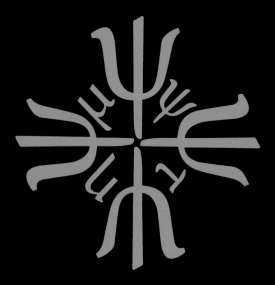

At this time there was a Titan named Atlas who ruled over the ends of the earth. King Atlas was powerful and vastly wealthy.

With Medusa vanquished, Perseus continued on his quest. He traveled as far as he could go, until he arrived at the western edge of the world.

He owned huge tracts of land that were unrivaled in their lush and fruitful beauty.

Of all the sprawling lands that Atlas owned, he treasured the Garden of Hesperides the most. The garden contained a tree of golden apples.

Perseus arrived at Atlas's gates, weary and hungry from the long journey. He asked Atlas for food and shelter so he could rest and regain his strength.

But the great Titan would not help. He had been told a prophecy that a descendent of Zeus would arrive at his garden and steal the precious golden apples.

Atlas turned Perseus away, throwing him from the gates in the process.

Shocked and angered by Atlas's treatment of him, Perseus pulled the head of Medusa out of the bag that he had been carrying.

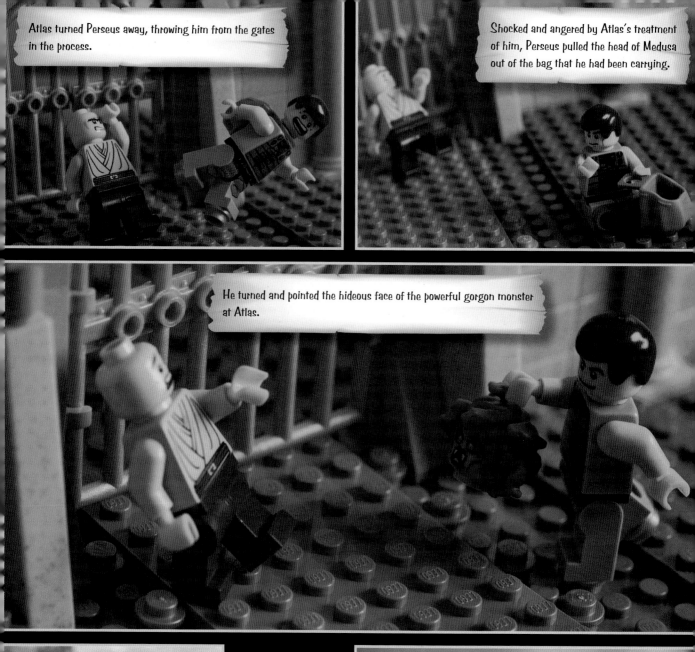

He turned and pointed the hideous face of the powerful gorgon monster at Atlas.

Atlas was immediately turned to stone, and with that, the great Mount Atlas was formed. The weight of the sky and the stars would be forever planted on his shoulders.

Safe from harm, Perseus continued his quest, using the winged sandals gifted to him by Hermes to fly off to Ethiopia.

Perseus and Andromeda

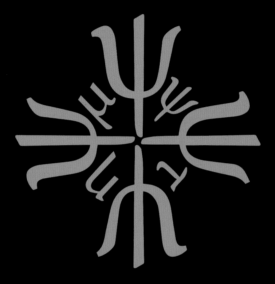

Perseus continued on his great quest, flying over the seas by way of his winged sandals.

On his journey, he glanced down and saw a woman chained to a rock.

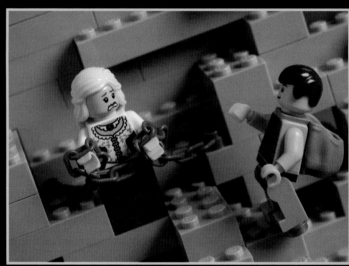

He almost continued on his way, thinking that she was a statue, but her hair blew in the breeze and Perseus saw how lovely she was.

He flew down to her and asked her what had happened.

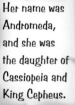

Her name was Andromeda, and she was the daughter of Cassiopeia and King Cepheus.

Andromeda explained that her mother had been exceedingly boastful, claiming that she and Andromeda were more beautiful than even the fairest of the Neired sea nymphs.

This insulted the Neireds, who felt Cassiopeia's hubris deserved retribution.

The sea nymphs brought their concerns to Poseidon.

Hearing the Neireds tell their story, Poseidon became angered and annoyed by Cassiopeia's mortal vanity.

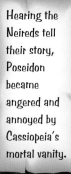

In response, he first flooded the lands that Cassiopeia and King Cepheus ruled over.

Then he unleashed a great sea monster in the form of a serpent, sending it to avenge the Neireds.

The sea monster caused immense destruction.

Not knowing what to do, King Cepheus sought the advice of an oracle to help ward off the beast. The oracle told him that he must offer the sea monster his daughter, Andromeda, in sacrifice.

King Cepheus was torn and could not imagine doing such a thing to his daughter. But the pressure from his subjects was too heavy, and he reluctantly agreed to sacrifice Andromeda, chaining her to the rock where Perseus had discovered her.

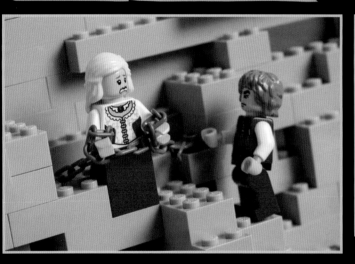

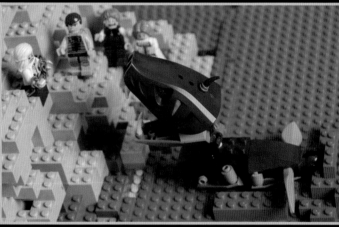

Andromeda finished telling her story and Perseus understood how terrible her situation was.

Suddenly, Andromeda's parents appeared on the rock, and the ocean began to churn and swell. From the depths of the sea, out came the horrific serpent, baring its razor-like teeth.

Perseus told him that if he would give him permission to marry the girl, he would save Andromeda. King Cepheus agreed to Perseus's terms.

Andromeda's father became hysterical with fear and worry.

Perseus flew up to the monster, wielding his sharp sword in front of him.

He slashed the creature,

cutting him into pieces.

When they returned home and were safe, Andromeda and Perseus were married.

Cassiopeia and King Cepheus offered the couple the whole of their kingdom to rule over.

They all lived happily, except for Cassiopeia, who was still punished. Poseidon transformed her into a cluster of stars and scattered her across the sky.

Perseus and the Prophecy

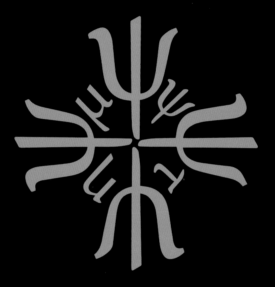

After a jubilant wedding, Perseus and Andromeda continued along their travels.

They stopped in Larisa, where there was a great festival of games and competitions. Perseus decided to enter into the games.

Little did Perseus know, his grandfather, Acrisius, had been hiding out in the very same city and was attending the very same games.

Perseus began the games by joining the discus-throwing competition. He threw the discus with great strength.

Unfortunately, the discus veered off course and struck Acrisius in the head.

Acrisius died instantly, fulfilling the prophecy he had feared from so long ago.

Perseus discovered what he had done, and to whom, and became distraught. He buried his grandfather with a heavy heart.

After this terrible event, Andromeda and Perseus decided to return from the quest and bring the head of Medusa to Polydectes.

Upon their arrival, they encountered Dictys, the fisherman brother who had saved Danae and baby Perseus from so many years before.

Dictys told Perseus that Polydectes had tricked him. The wedding had been a farce, and Danae had been forced to act as Polydectes's servant while Perseus was away.

Perseus was horrorstruck. He had left his mother at the mercy of Polydectes and unintentionally caused her to suffer hardship while he went on his exciting journey.

Furious, Perseus stormed the palace to confront Polydectes. As he entered, he warned his mother to move out of the way and close her eyes.

From his bag he pulled out Medusa's hideous head and unleashed her powers of destruction.

Polydectes and his men were caught off guard and shrieked in horror as Perseus stood before them with the gorgon head.

Each was turned to stone forever, and Perseus was victorious.

Artemis and Apollo

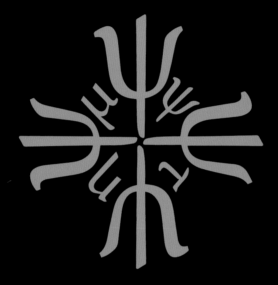

Artemis and Apollo were twin gods, born to Zeus and Leto.

Leto's pregnancy had been difficult. Hera had been jealous of her relationship with Zeus and had sent a serpent to chase and harass Leto.

The serpent followed Leto across the earth, preventing her from finding a safe place to rest and bear her children.

Finally Leto found refuge on an island and began to give birth.

Artemis was born first and immediately began aiding her mother through her labor, acting as her midwife.

With Artemis's help, Leto gave birth to Apollo. Thus Artemis became a patron goddess of childbirth, as well as virginity, guardian of young girls, and helper of women.

Artemis was also the goddess of the hunt, the wilderness, and wild animals. Zeus was delighted with his daughter and gave her whatever she wanted. At her request, he gave her permission to never marry and remain a maiden forever. He gave her the wild mountains to watch over as her domain and had a beautiful silver bow and arrows made for her.

Apollo was also one of his father's favorites. He was a handsome young man and powerful god, and he was renowned for his skill in music, poetry, and philosophy.

The twins grew to be skilled archers and hunters at a young age.

They were devoted to their mother and remained grateful to her for suffering through their difficult birth.

Apollo sought the serpent that had chased Leto during her pregnancy and killed it with his spear.

Once, a giant named Tityus tried to steal Leto and take her as his wife.

Leto fled and called to her children for help.

Artemis and Apollo ran to their mother's side, and together they slayed the monstrous foe.

Zeus then banished the giant to eternal torture in the Underworld for good measure.

At this time there lived a woman named Niobe who was queen of Thebes and the daughter of Tantalus. Niobe refused to honor Leto or Artemis and Apollo at Leto's temple.

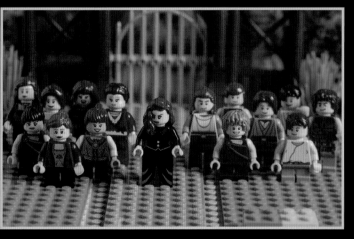

Niobe had children of her own: seven sons and seven daughters. She proclaimed that she was a better mother than Leto, and so she refused to worship the goddess.

Leto was greatly offended by Niobe's boastful words, and she told her children to defend her and her honor.

The twins agreed and set out to punish Niobe.

They found Niobe's sons at play by the front gate and crept up silently behind them.

Together they unleashed a torrent of arrows onto the boys' heads.

When it was over they had killed all seven of Niobe's sons.

Niobe came, and when she saw what had happened she cried out in anguish. She cursed cruel Leto and told her she had won their contest.

Then in fury she relented, and again challenged the goddess. Niobe said that she still had seven daughters, which was more children than Leto, and so she was still the best mother.

The sisters came out to see what had happened and saw their brothers dead on the ground.

From their perch, Artemis and Apollo shot at them with arrows.

Soon all but the youngest daughter was dead.

Niobe begged for them to spare her youngest child.

But it was too late.

Niobe was consumed by her grief at the loss of her children. Her sorrow was so great that she was transformed into a statue that would cry for the rest of eternity.

Artemis and Orion

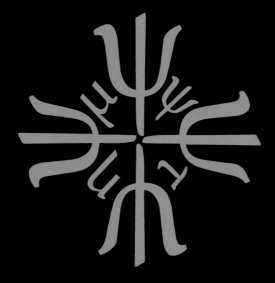

As Artemis and Apollo got older, Artemis began spending more time with her friend Orion, who was Poseidon's son. Orion was a strong, handsome man and a skilled hunter.

Apollo felt left out and was jealous of their close friendship. This made him angry, and he decided to punish Artemis and Orion.

Meanwhile Apollo challenged Artemis to an archery contest.

The next day, Orion took a swim in the river before he was to meet Artemis for their daily hunt.

He pointed out at the water where Orion swam far off in the distance, too far to see him clearly. Orion's head looked just like a rock sticking out of the water. Apollo said that whoever managed to hit the rock would be the winner of their contest.

So Artemis drew her bow and let fly an arrow, faster and straighter than any mortal on earth could shoot.

The goddess's aim was true, and she struck her friend on the head, killing him.

When his body floated to shore, Artemis was heartbroken. As a reward for his loyalty and companionship, she put his body into the sky as a constellation, and there it remains as a tribute to their friendship.

Artemis and Actaeon

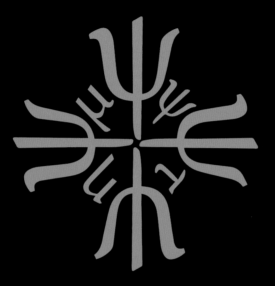

Actaeon was a man who did not fare as well in his dealings with Artemis. He was the grandson of King Cadmus of Thebes, and it was well known that he was a handsome young man and a brave hunter.

One day when Actaeon was out hunting, he wandered off away from his friends.

There he stumbled upon the goddess Artemis bathing. Her nymph handmaidens tried to shield her from his sight, but they were not fast enough.

In his wanderings, he found a lovely cool spring. It was so sweet and refreshing that he waded in.

Artemis was embarrassed and infuriated by this disturbance.

Actaeon had seen her radiant beauty, completely unrobed.

She tried to reach for her bow, but it was too far away.

When the water touched him, he was transformed into a deer. Frightened, Actaeon turned his fluffy tail and fled into the forest.

His own hunting dogs caught his new scent, and soon they chased him down and tore him to pieces. And this was his punishment for spying on the terrible, beautiful goddess.

Atalanta

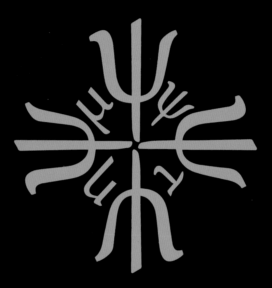

There was once an Arkadian huntress who was smart and strong. Her name was Atalanta, and she was well loved by the goddess Artemis.

When Atalanta was an infant, her father, Iasios, had left her to die in the forest. He had decided that he wanted only sons for children.

The bear cared for the baby until she grew bigger and stronger.

A motherly bear came upon Atalanta and took her in.

Eventually, Atalanta was found by hunters, who raised her as their own for the rest of her childhood.

Atalanta grew up to be a fierce and independent young woman, one who did not need a partner to provide for her. She could do it on her own.

She would have none of it, and she shot him with her arrows.

She came upon a centaur, who tried in vain to court her.

Later, she asked Jason if she could join the Argonauts. She wanted to be a part of the powerful group and have her chance at hunting the Calydonian boar. The Argonauts balked at the idea of a woman hunter and said no.

Atalanta ignored them and joined the hunt anyway. With her cunning and hunting prowess, she was the first to draw blood from the massive boar.

Meleager, a member of the Argonauts, skinned the boar and tried to give the hide to Atalanta as a trophy for her accomplishment.

The other men were angered by this, so a perilous fight broke out and all the men were killed.

At the funerals, traditional games and competitions were held in the men's honor. Atalanta entered a wrestling contest and came out victorious. Her notoriety spread, and she was now someone people recognized as a valiant huntress.

She became so well regarded that her father returned, asking for her to come back home with him.

When she returned with him, he insisted that she marry.

Atalanta was about to the refuse outright, but instead she placed a bet with her father. If a suitor were able to beat her in a footrace, then he would have the privilege of marrying her. If he failed, she would cut off his head.

For a while, this arrangement worked out very well for Atalanta.

Many men took on the challenge of the footrace, wishing to make Atalanta their bride. None of the suitors could outrun her, and as promised, she swiftly beheaded them.

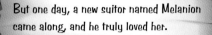

But one day, a new suitor named Melanion came along, and he truly loved her.

He knew he was no match for Atalanta, and that if he tried to race her on his own, he would be sure to lose. He prayed to Aphrodite for her help in winning the race.

Aphrodite listened to Melanion's request and agreed to help him. She gave him three golden apples and told him to use them during the race to help distract Atalanta.

This offer of assistance did not come without a price. Aphrodite made Melanion promise that, in return, he must make a sacrifice to Aphrodite when the race was over.

Melanion eagerly agreed and went off to win over Atalanta. During the race, he threw one of the golden apples down the path ahead. Atalanta saw the golden apple and picked it up.

She knew that she was a far stronger runner than her opponent, and she quickly caught up with him.

Melanion threw the second apple, and again, Atalanta stopped to pick it up.

She once again caught up to Melanion, just as they were coming in to the finish of the race. He threw the final apple, and she stopped to pick that one up as well.

Atalanta was so distracted by the bright golden apples that she didn't realize they had cost her the race. Melanion victoriously crossed the finish line.

Melanion was overjoyed; he got to keep his head and he had proved himself worthy of marrying the powerful and beautiful huntress. He was so elated that he forgot the promise he made to Aphrodite.

Atalanta found that she was actually quite fond of Melanion. She and her new husband went to a sacred shrine devoted to Zeus. They began to kiss, which was strictly forbidden in the temple.

Aphrodite saw them together and became enraged, for Melanion's neglect of their bargain felt like an affront to her power.

So Aphrodite used her godly powers against the new lovers.

And she turned them into lions, because it was believed that lions could not mate with one another. From then on, Atalanta and Melanion could never be together.

The Minotaur

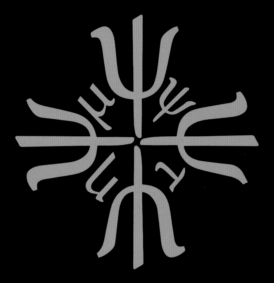

King Minos of the island of Crete was worried and wished to make his claim to the throne more secure. So he promised Poseidon that he would make a great and wonderful sacrifice in the god's honor. He vowed that he would sacrifice whatever creature the god would send him from the sea.

Poseidon sent a great bull for Minos to sacrifice, but when the king saw the beast, he declared that it was too beautiful to kill.

So he secretly found a different bull and sacrificed the creature for Poseidon.

Poseidon was not fooled by this trick, and he was furious at Minos's betrayal!

He filled the real bull with rage and sent it rampaging across Crete.

It ran through the countryside and through the villages, destroying everything in its path.

Poseidon even bewitched Minos's wife Pasiphae to fall in love with the creature in revenge for Minos's betrayal.

Around this time, the famous sculptor Daedulus and his son Icarus arrived in Crete, fleeing persecution for the murder of Daedulus's nephew. King Minos invited them into his house warmly, happy to have suck a skilled artist at hand.

Pasiphae was so moved by her love for the beast, she went to Daedalus to ask for his help.

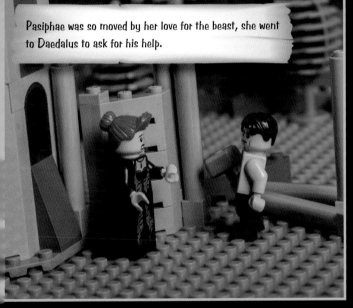

The artist fashioned her a clever cow disguise and helped her to hide inside of it.

The disguise fooled the bull, and the beast soon became enamored with the queen.

Pasiphae became pregnant with the bull's offspring and gave birth to a strange half-bull, half-man creature that they called the Minotaur. She named her child Asterion.

Enraged, Minos enslaved Daedalus and Icarus for helping Pasiphae carry out her affair.

As Asterion grew, he became wilder and wilder, like his father. He began devouring people, and the people of Crete were afraid for their lives.

Meanwhile, King Minos's son Andogoes was killed in battle by the Athenians.

Minos brought Daedalus from prison and ordered him to construct a great labyrinth for the creature. When the labyrinth was finished, they sent the Minotaur to the very center to live.

In revenge for the death of his only human son, King Minos demanded that Athens send him a tribute of Athenian children: every nine years they must send him seven girls and seven boys. Each year of the tribute, these children of Athens were sent into the labyrinth to feed the Minotaur, and he would devour each one.

On the third year of these tributes, young Theseus, son of King Aegeus of Athens, stepped forward to volunteer himself for tribute.

His father begged and pleaded and commanded him to stay, but Theseus was determined to make his name as a hero.

He told his father that he would slay the beast and put an end to the tributes. If he were successful, he would signal to his father by sailing home with white sails raised. If he failed and was killed, the ship would return home with black sails.

Theseus arrived in Crete along with the other young people sent as tribute for the Minotaur.

When King Minos's daughter Ariadne saw Theseus among the crowd, she instantly fell in love with the handsome youth.

Fearing that Theseus would be killed by her half brother the Minotaur, Ariadne went to Daedalus to ask him how Theseus could escape the labyrinth.

Daedalus instructed her to give Theseus string to mark his path so that he could find his way out of the labyrinth once he had killed the beast.

Ariadne went to Theseus and told him she could help him escape the labyrinth. However, she would only share her secret if Theseus promised to take her back to Athens and make her his queen.

Theseus happily agreed to marry the beautiful Ariadne, and she gave him the spool of string, instructing him to use it to mark his path.

The day soon came, and the tributes were sent into the labyrinth to meet their end at the Minotaur's jaws. Theseus brought his spool of thread along with him.

Before he continued into the labyrinth, he tied the end of the string to the door.

Then he began to make his way through the maze, unraveling the spool as he went. All through the labyrinth he saw evidence of the Minotaur's ravenous appetite.

Finally he came to the center, where he found the monster sleeping.

Theseus moved quickly, ran over to the beast, and pulled off its horn.

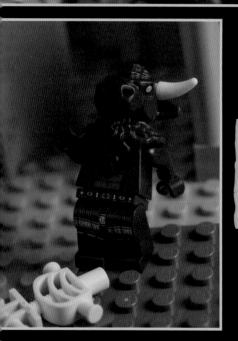

The monster bellowed in pain and fury and prepared to charge!

Theseus stood far enough back, and he raised the Minotaur's horn in his hand like a javelin.

Then he threw the horn hard, sending it straight through the Minotaur's heart to kill him.

Theseus called to the other Athenian youths, and they all followed his spool of thread to find their way out of the labyrinth.

Everyone was happy to have survived the ordeal, and they thanked Theseus profusely.

The Athenians set out for home, and as he promised, Theseus took Ariadne with him.

On their way, they stopped at the beautiful island of Naxos and had a loud, long celebration.

Ariadne laid out in the sand for a nap, and while she was sleeping, the party packed up and boarded the ship, unknowingly leaving her behind.

Theseus was heartbroken when he realized that she was missing, but it was too late to turn back.

Because the young hero was so upset about the loss of his beautiful bride, he forgot the promise he had made to his father to signal his successful return by raising the white sails.

When King Aegeus of Athens saw his ship returning with the black sails raised, he was filled with pain and grief, thinking his son was surely dead.

In his sorrow, the King threw himself from the top of a cliff into the sea.

Daedalus and Icarus

There was once a very skilled craftsman named Daedalus.

He was an architect and a sculptor, whose talent for great art was unmatched by anyone in the world.

The statues and sculptures that Daedalus crafted were so lifelike—with gazing eyes and limbs that looked like they were in motion—that many people believed the statues were secretly animated and could spring to life. But with this great talent came a great fear; Daedalus often worried that another artist would prove to be better than him.

This fear ate at him, even when he mentored his own nephew, Talus.

As it turned out, Talus developed into an incredible sculptor and inventor in his own right. Word spread of Talus's skill, and some even said he was better than Daedalus.

With his fears coming true, Daedalus decided he had to do something to stop Talus from becoming a greater and more famous artist.

So Daedalus made a plan to get rid of him. He took Talus to the very top of the Acropolis and threw him off, sending the young sculptor plummeting to his untimely death.

Then, to hide his crime, he began to dig a grave to bury the boy. He dug and dug until he had a Talus-sized grave prepared.

As he sifted through the dirt and scattered it over Talus, a curious onlooker came by and noticed what he was doing. In horror, the witness cried, "MURDER!" and Daedalus knew he had been caught.

Narrowly escaping capture, Daedalus fled, taking a boat to the nearby island of Crete.

When Daedalus arrived in Crete, King Minos greeted him warmly, for he had great respect for his art and treated him as a friend.

Not wasting any time with such a skilled craftsman in his presence, King Minos quickly put Daedalus to work, asking him to build a vast and complex labyrinth.

Daedalus worked tirelessly, completing what would be his greatest structure yet. The labyrinth was vast and winding, and only he knew how to navigate it.

Once the labyrinth was complete, King Minos imprisoned the Minotaur—half man, half bull—in the center of the inescapable maze.

Despite his great accomplishments on Crete, Daedalus grew tired and homesick from living on a faraway island.

Knowing that Daedalus held the key to the labyrinth's mysteries and that he could one day betray him, King Minos refused to let Daedalus leave. Enraged, Daedalus told King Minos that while he may be able to prevent him from leaving by land or by sea, there was one area he could not rule over.

Daedalus and his son, Icarus, worked together to plan their escape from Crete, deciding that if they could not escape by land or by sea, they would go by air.

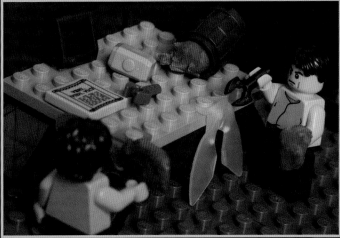

Being a great sculptor, Daedalus fashioned pairs of wings with wax and feathers.

He gave a pair to Icarus so that they could fly away together.

Before leaving, Daedalus warned Icarus that he must always fly along the same path as his father. If he flew too low, his wings would become wet with the spray of the sea and he would drown. If he flew too high, the heat of the sun would melt the wax and his wings would be destroyed. Icarus readily agreed and promised his father that he would stay close to him.

Daedalus and Icarus took off, ready to leave Crete far behind them.

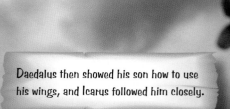

Daedalus then showed his son how to use his wings, and Icarus followed him closely.

Growing bold and ignoring his father's warnings, Icarus flew away from Daedalus, soaring up and down through the sky.

Icarus felt elated and free and rose higher and higher through the clouds toward the gleaming sun. He was so excited by his flight, however, that he didn't notice that the wax on his wings had begun to melt, dripping down to the sea below.

The wax melted and his wings broke apart, causing Icarus to plunge from the bright sky and into the sea.

Daedalus, realizing too late that his son was no longer following him, frantically scanned the sky.

Looking down at the sea, Daedalus watched as the broken and melted wings were swallowed by the ocean below.

Struck by terror and grief, he cried out for his son.

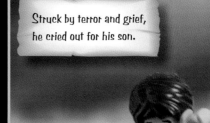

Hubris had killed Icarus, for he was too proud and overconfident to listen to his father about flying too close to the sun.

Overwhelmed with grief, Daedalus landed in Sicily where King Cocalus welcomed him.

Daedalus built an impenetrable wall for King Cocalus so that the king could protect his wares and treasures.

Meanwhile, back in Crete, King Minos had not forgotten Daedalus's escape and the important secret he held.

King Minos traveled to Sicily and sent a messenger to King Cocalus to demand he be told the whereabouts of Daedalus.

King Cocalus did not take kindly to King Minos's threats and became greatly angered.

He did not take this competition for the great artist lightly and began plotting ways to destroy King Minos.

Solidifying his plan, King Cocalus pretended to agree to King Minos's wishes and give up Daedalus. He welcomed King Minos and his guards into the walls of his city.

Offering King Minos a bit of respite after his long travels, King Cocalus instructed his daughters to draw Minos a warm bath.

Little did he know, King Cocalus had also told his daughters to heat the water until King Minos was boiled alive.

King Cocalus delivered the bad news to King Minos's men that he had died, explaining that he had slipped and fallen into the tub.

Though he had escaped capture from his enemies, Daedalus mourned his son to the end of his days.

Now safe from King Minos, Daedalus lived and worked freely in Sicily, even founding a school of sculpture to teach future generations his fine craft.

Tantalus

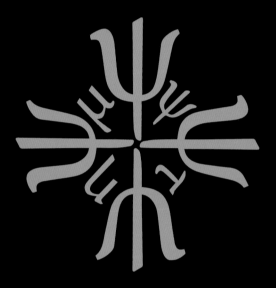

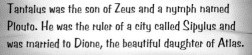

Tantalus was the son of Zeus and a nymph named Plouto. He was the ruler of a city called Sipylus and was married to Dione, the beautiful daughter of Atlas.

Tantalus was well known for being a very rich man.

Because of his wealth, he was well liked by the gods and was often invited to dine with them at their great feasts on Mount Olympus.

But Tantalus took advantage of this great privilege. First, he stole ambrosia, the precious food of the immortals, from the gods at one of the feasts.

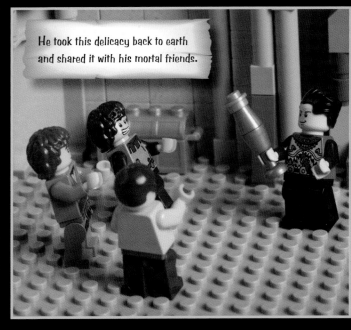

He took this delicacy back to earth and shared it with his mortal friends.

Tantalus also listened closely to the talk of the gods while dining with them, taking note of all their gossip and secrets.

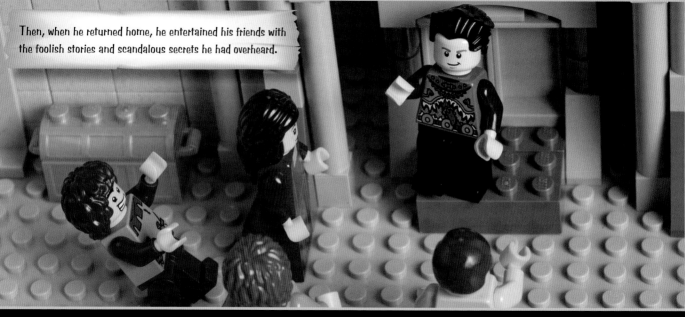

Then, when he returned home, he entertained his friends with the foolish stories and scandalous secrets he had overheard.

Tantalus was also involved in the disappearance of Zeus's golden dog, which was created by Hephaestus at Zeus's birth to take care of the newborn god.

Tantalus was given the dog for safekeeping, but when asked to return him, he claimed he had never heard of such a dog.

The gods, taking note of Tantalus's bad behavior, decided to forgo punishing him for now and give the rich man another chance to earn their favor.

Tantalus then invited the gods to dine with him. He had a plan and intended to test the gods on their intelligence and powers of observation.

In preparation for this dinner party, Tantalus killed his own son, Pelops. He then cut the boy up and put him into the soup to serve to the gods.

The gods realized what he had done and refused to eat.

None of the gods took even a bite, save for Demeter, who was sad and distracted by the loss of her daughter. She ate a small part of the boy's shoulder before she realized what was in front of her.

Zeus was able to reassemble the child, replacing his missing shoulder with a new one crafted from ivory. Then he brought the boy back to life.

As terrible as it was for Tantalus to insult the gods, killing his son and serving him was much worse. For his many dreadful offenses, the gods sent him to the Underworld with Hades for a particularly clever punishment.

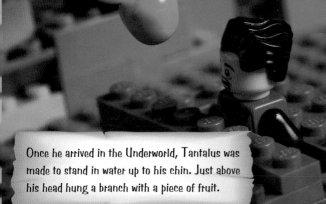

Once he arrived in the Underworld, Tantalus was made to stand in water up to his chin. Just above his head hung a branch with a piece of fruit.

If ever he reached for the sweet ripe fruit, the branch would pull and stretch away from him, keeping the food just beyond his reach, and whenever he would stoop to take a drink of water, it receded into the ground, just beyond his grasp.

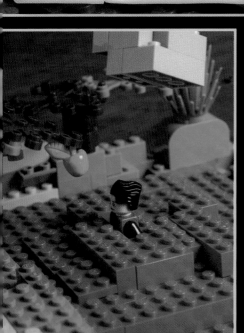

Above him hung a huge boulder that threatened to come down on his head at any moment.

Here he remained for eternity, with all his wants within sight but always just beyond his reach.

Sisyphus

Sisyphus was the founder and king of the great city of Corinth.

He was widely known as being very cunning. If there was ever a problem, he always knew the cleverest way to fix it.

One day, Sisyphus discovered that a bandit named Autolycus had been stealing all of his livestock.

Sisyphus could never prove that Autolycus was the thief, because Autolycus had an amazing power that allowed him to transform all of the pigs and goats and sheep to other colors and other animals.

Finally, Sisyphus had an idea. He marked the hooves of all his livestock so that, even if they were turned into different animals, he would know that they were his.

The next time Autolycus stole his animals, Sisyphus was able to prove that each were one of his by showing the marks on their hooves. The dastardly thief was sent away in chains.

While Sisyphus was famous for his craftiness in situations like these, he was notorious for darker deeds. He was unabashedly deceitful, and he took pleasure in killing travelers and stealing the daughters of his enemies to maintain his power.

If it suited him, he would even dare to cheat the gods.

The river god Asopus, who was the son of Poseidon, sought help from Sisyphus. He had searched high and low, far and wide, and could not find his beloved daughter, Aegina.

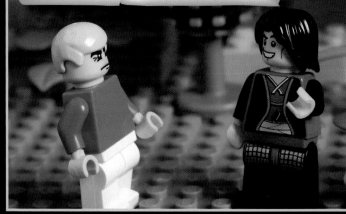

Sisyphus, seeing the profit that could come from the man's desperation, told Asopus that he would help him on one condition. If Asopus would build Sisyphus an eternal spring, Sisyphus would come to his aid.

The grieving father readily agreed and built Sisyphus a beautiful and unending spring.

Sisyphus made good on his promise and told Asopus that it was Zeus who had taken his daughter.

Overhearing this, Zeus became enraged at the betrayal. Sisyphus had told the truth, but Zeus would not allow his secrets to be spread.

So he sent Thanatos, the god of death, to punish and kill Sisyphus for revealing his deeds.

Thanatos found Sisyphus. And he had brought along handcuffs with which to ensnare Sisyphus and bring him to the Underworld.

Being the cunning man he was, Sisyphus had an idea. He asked Thanatos to demonstrate how the chains worked.

Thanatos snapped the handcuffs over his own wrists, showing Sisyphus how very well they worked.

Seizing his opportunity, Sisyphus captured the chained Thanatos and imprisoned him in a closet. The god of death, whose job it was to escort the dead to the Underworld, was now faced with a problem.

Those who died could no longer be transported to the afterlife, which meant that, no matter how gruesome the death, the dead were forced to linger in the living world.

Eventually, Ares, the god of war, discovered what was happening and freed Thanatos from Sisyphus's capture.

Together, Thanatos and Ares brought Sisyphus to the Underworld.

But not before Sisyphus had the chance to try one last plan. He plotted with his wife, telling her to do him a favor.

The clever man told her not to give him a proper burial, nor to prepare a funeral feast, nor to put a coin under his tongue as payment to Charon, the ferryman who carries the dead across the river Styx.

When Sisyphus arrived in the Underworld, he pleaded to Persephone for her understanding. He feigned horror when he told her her that his terrible wife had refused to give him proper funeral rites.

He begged her to give him permission to return to the mortal world for three days. This would give Sisyphus time to be buried properly and return to the Underworld justly.

Persephone, who was a compassionate queen of the Underworld, said yes, giving him permission for the three days—and the three days only.

Of course, the deceitful Sisyphus had cleverly fooled Persephone, with no plans to fulfill his promise of return. He rode back across the river Styx to the world of the living.

Sisyphus lived for many more years, until he was an old man.

Upon his death, he returned to the Underworld to meet the wrath of Hades, who condemned him to an eternity of hard labor.

He was damned to roll a heavy boulder to the top of a high and treacherous mountain.

Each time Sisyphus reached the summit of the mountain, tired, panting, and aching from his efforts . . .

. . . the boulder thundered right back down the base, where he was doomed to start over again.

Marathon

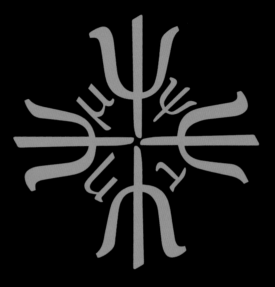

There was once a time in the history of Greece when the Persian Empire threatened to conquer all of the Greek city-states.

The Greeks vowed to resist their invasion, but the Persian army was strong, and the Greeks watched as the Persian force swept closer, burning and enslaving neighboring islands and city-states in its wake.

At last the Persian army arrived in Greece, landing on the shores of the city of Marathon, just north of Athens.

When the Greeks saw the Persians preparing for battle, they realized that they were greatly outnumbered.

The Athenian general in charge of the troops decided to send someone to the Spartans and ask for their help. He chose to send a man named Pheidippides, who was widely considered the most athletic soldier.

Pheidippides proudly accepted the task and set off for Sparta.

He ran all 140 miles through rocky and rugged terrain.

When he arrived in Sparta, they welcomed him, and they told him they would gladly send their soldiers to defend their neighbor, but it would have to wait until after they had finished their religious festival.

So Pheidippides returned to Marathon.

He found the Athenian general and told him the unfortunate news: the reinforcements were delayed.

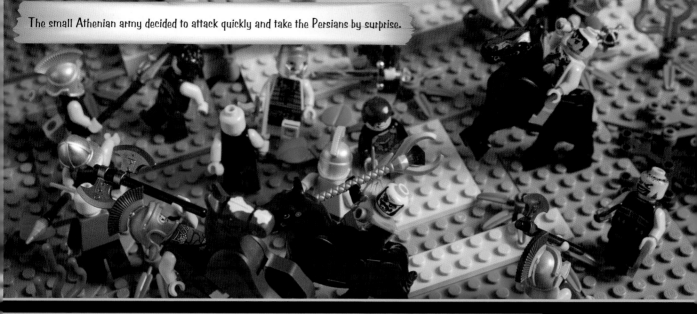

The small Athenian army decided to attack quickly and take the Persians by surprise.

And so the Athenians marched on the much bigger Persian army and began to fight. Although they were greatly outnumbered, the Athenians used speed and clever tactics to gain an advantage.

When the battle was over, the Athenians were victorious! They had managed to beat the Persian army, sustaining only 200 casualties, while the Persians had lost 6,500 soldiers.

But the threat was not over. The surviving Persians regrouped and headed south by sea to strike the undefended city of Athens.

As he ran, he shouted "Nike! Nike!" which meant victory. He arrived in Athens and successfully delivered his message.

Swift Pheidippides was sent to Athens to share the news of the army's victory and to warn them of the impending attack.

Then he fell down dead of exhaustion, with the word "victory" still on his lips.

Meanwhile the Athenian army, still weary from their battle, marched swiftly from Marathon to reach Athens, outfitted in heavy armor and carrying their weighty swords. This feat is considered the first marathon race in history.

The Athenian army arrived in the city and beat back the invaders.

The Spartan army arrived as well, and together the Greeks routed the Persian army, pushing them back until they fled toward their own shores.

Narcissus

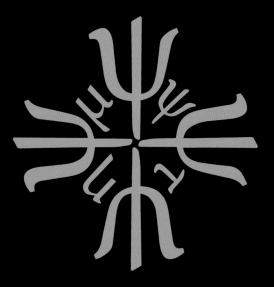

Narcissus was the son of a river god and a nymph.

Far and wide, he was renowned for his handsome looks.

Although Narcissus was attractive on the outside, he was not so beautiful on the inside. He was very arrogant and often rude to those who admired him.

One day when he was walking in the woods, Narcissus caught the attention of a lovely mountain nymph named Echo. Echo fell deeply in love with him.

Echo was a loquacious nymph, notorious for her constant banter and conversation.

She was a bit mischievous, as well. She once used her powers of chatter to help an unfaithful god escape his wife.

When the goddess discovered the betrayal and Echo's part in it, she punished her to live forever without the gift of conversation. From then on, Echo could only repeat what was spoken to her.

Echo waited in the woods near Narcissus, desperately trying to figure out a way to express her love for him. She felt trapped, because she knew she could only repeat the words he spoke to her.

Not knowing what else to do, Echo approached Narcissus and tried to embrace him.

Narcissus pushed the nymph away from him. Grief-stricken, she retreated back into the woods.

Echo ran to the mountains, where she eventually died of heartbreak.

Upon her death, she became a part of the stone in the mountain. Her voice remained, only to be heard as an echo.

Narcissus did not notice the harm he had done to Echo. He continued to reject fair nymphs who crossed his path, indifferent to their feelings.

This angered the gods, who had been watching Narcissus.

They decided to punish him, cursing him to fall in love with someone or something that could not love him back.

Soon after, the vain Narcissus happened upon a pond. There he saw his own reflection and became enamored with it.

Narcissus fell so deeply in love with his own reflection that he tried to kiss it.

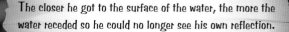

The closer he got to the surface of the water, the more the water receded so he could no longer see his own reflection.

Narcissus spent the rest of his life pining away at his likeness in the water, distraught over what he could not have.

Taking pity on him, the mountain nymphs turned Narcissus into a beautiful flower.

Heracles: The Birth of the Divine Hero

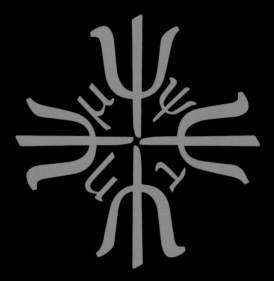

Heracles was the son of Zeus and the mortal woman Alcmene.

When Heracles was very small, Alcmene feared that Hera would harm him if he stayed in the palace, so she left him in a field by himself.

Athena and Hera happened upon the suffering Heracles in the field and felt sorry for him.

Not knowing whom the baby was, Hera nursed him back to life. Because she was a great goddess, this action transferred supernatural powers to baby Heracles.

Athena then took him to a nearby city.

157

She asked the queen of the city to take care of the baby.

Alcmene looked on, and it dawned on her that the boy was her child. She was overjoyed that he had survived.

When she realized that the baby she had saved was Zeus's illegitimate son, Hera was infuriated that she had let go of her chance to kill him.

She sent a venomous serpent to Heracles's crib to kill him in his sleep.

But baby Heracles had acquired incredible strength and powers, and he played with the snake as if it were a rattle.

Heracles's new guardian, King Amphitryon, knew that Heracles's superhuman strength meant he was very special.

So he called upon Tiresias, a seer, to look into Heracles's future.

Tiresias's prophecy foresaw that Heracles would become a great champion and slayer of beasts, and that he would become immortal.

Knowing the incredible destiny that laid ahead of Heracles, King Amphitryon decided to give him the best education possible to prepare him.

Amphitryon showed Heracles how to drive a chariot.

He introduced him to archery.

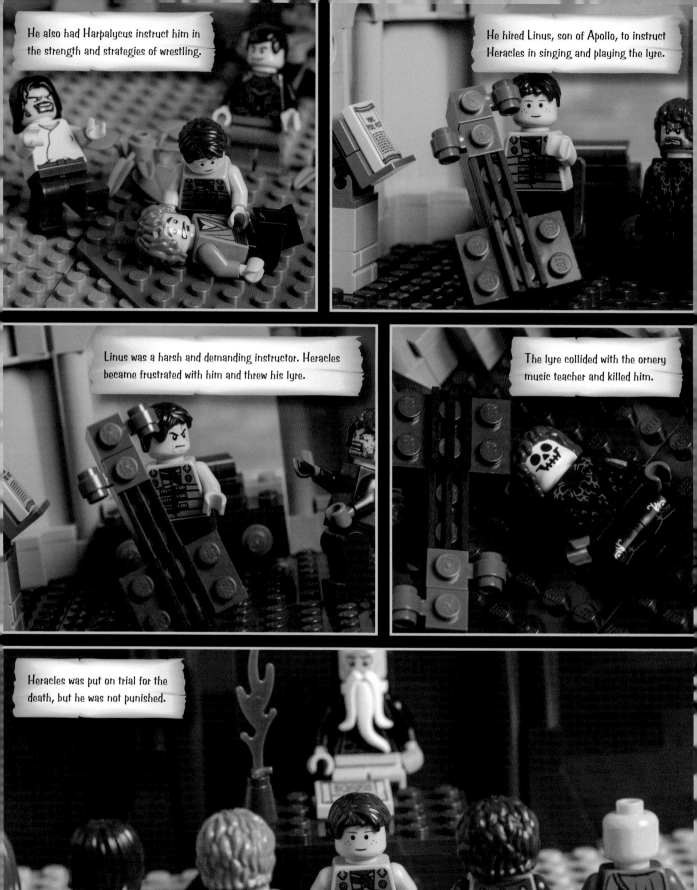

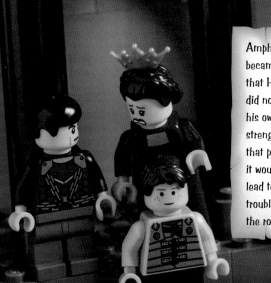

Amphitryon became afraid that Heracles did not know his own strength, and that perhaps it would lead to more trouble down the road.

He sent him to the countryside to learn the ways of farming and to tend to livestock with other shepherds.

During this time, Heracles grew to be exceedingly handsome and strong.

When he came of age, Heracles left the shepherds to go off on his own.

He came upon two desirable nymphs who were Pleasure and Virtue.

The first nymph, Pleasure, told him that he could choose between the two of them, for they represented the path he would take in life.

She explained that if he chose her, Heracles would be free of hardship, war, and the burdens of unhappiness.

Heracles turned to the other woman, Virtue, to hear what she had to say.

She told him that with her, Heracles would become a great hero of Greece, and one who would win the favor and admiration of the gods. But this would only come with hard work, immense toil, and sometimes great suffering.

Heracles thought deeply about his choice and decided to take the path of Virtue.

To begin his noble trek, Heracles decided to rid the lands of Greece of all of the savage beasts, ne'er-do-wellers, and thieves that corrupted it.

First, he hunted down an enormous lion in his lair on Mount Cithaeron.

Heracles killed the lion with his mighty club.

And then made a protective cloak out of its hide.

Donning the pelt of the lion, Heracles ran into an unsavory messenger of Erginus, King of the Minyans.

The messenger was sent to capture Theban tributes for a deadly annual tournament.

Angered by the dark intentions, Heracles attacked the messenger, injuring him.

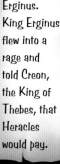

Outfitted with many wounds and bandages, he sent the injured man back to King Erginus. King Erginus flew into a rage and told Creon, the King of Thebes, that Heracles would pay.

Heracles gathered men of Thebes and convinced them to join him in a battle against the Minyans.

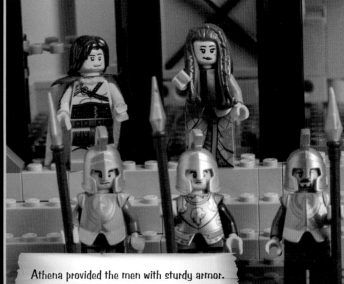

Athena provided the men with sturdy armor.

They fought the Minyans in a bloody battle.

Victoriously, Heracles killed the loathsome King Erignus. Sadly, the benevolent King Amphitryon was killed as well.

Devastated and vengeful, Heracles destroyed the Minyan's capitol.

He was celebrated all through Greece for his heroic actions.

King Creon, pleased with Heracles's defense of Thebes, allowed him to marry his beautiful daughter, Megara.

The gods also rewarded Heracles's gallant actions. Hermes gave him a mighty sword.

Apollo gave him the finest arrows.

Athena presented him with armor fit for a hero.

Heracles and Eurystheus

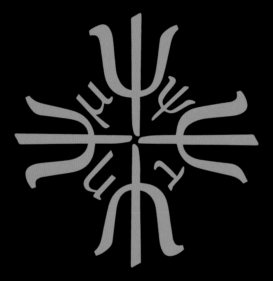

For a long while after, Heracles and Megara were blissful and had many children.

But Hera's hatred for Heracles continued to fester. She vowed to ruin his happiness and inflicted him with a burning and uncontrollable rage.

Maddened by the sorcery, Heracles terrorized his family and killed each of his children.

When the wave of anger subsided, Heracles fell into a great depression. Grief-stricken, he locked himself away so he could hurt no one.

After a time, Heracles sought the guidance of the Oracle of Delphi. He wished to atone for his horrific deeds.

The Oracle told Heracles that the only way he could repent would be to submit himself to King Eurystheus of Argos.

Little did Heracles know, at the time of his birth, Zeus had decreed that the first grandson of Perseus would rule over all of his descendants. Both Heracles and Eurystheus were in line for this title.

Not wanting the son of her rival to gain this power, Hera intervened during childbirth and Eurystheus arrived first.

Eurystheus became king but was always insecure about Heracles's great power and fame.

At the instruction of the Oracle of Delphi, Heracles presented himself to Eurystheus. The King commanded him to do ten impossible tasks to gain absolution for the slaughter of his children.

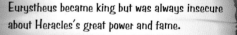

Proud Heracles was angered by the commands, feeling as if performing labors for the king were beneath him. At first, the petulant hero refused the tasks.

Eventually, the guilt of slaying his innocent children ate away at Heracles.

He returned to King Eurystheus and agreed to perform the tasks.

The Twelve Labors of Heracles

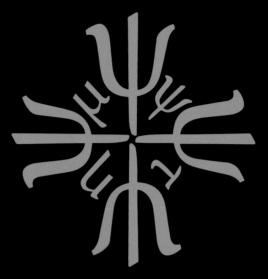

When Heracles finally accepted his ten labors, the first one was to slay the Nemean lion.

This giant beast was feared among all men. It could not be wounded by any man-made weapon, because it had impenetrable golden skin and its claws could tear through any armor.

Heracles began his search in a deep forest.

Late one night, when the moon was low and the forest was dark, Heracles discovered the Nemean lion sleeping near a cave. Heracles shot out an arrow to kill the lion, but the arrow bounced right off his impenetrable pelt.

Though the lion was not wounded, he was irritated with the attack. Spotting Heracles in the bushes, the lion pounced.

Heracles sprang into action and began attacking the lion with a heavy club.

Using his super strength, Heracles managed to strangle the lion to death.

He first tried to skin the lion using his sword, but it was to no avail. Heracles then tried using the lion's own claws and was able to remove the hide.

Eurystheus was so terrified by the feat that he hid in a cauldron.

Heracles returned to the palace having accomplished his first task, and he presented the skin of the lion to Eurystheus.

Second Labor

Heracles was ready to perform his second labor. This time, he was told to slay the Lernaean Hydra, which had been raised by Hera for the very purpose of killing Heracles. The hydra was a monstrous serpent that lived in a swamp and had three heads. Two of her heads were mortal and therefore could be killed. The middle head was deathless, which posed a problem for Heracles.

Heracles road on his chariot to seek out the Hydra.

When he finally found the terrifying beast, he lured her to him by shooting his arrows.

But for every time he did this, two new heads sprouted up.

The fight grew perilous. The Hydra snapped at his legs, biting him. In return, he bashed her head off with his club.

Heracles set the forest ablaze and burned the Hydra's heads before more could sprout back.

He climbed atop the great beast and began attacking the immortal head.

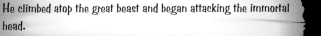

Heracles severed the immortal head from the Hydra's body.

Knowing that the head would not die, he buried it deep in the ground and rolled a massive bolder and many rocks over the spot.

Heracles saw the Hydra's venomous blood pool around the serpent's dead body. He dipped his arrowheads into the blood, coating them with the venom so that all those he shot with his arrows would be poisoned.

Third Labor

Heracles's third task was to capture the elusive Golden Hind of Artemis.

He followed the sacred deer on Mount Cerynea for over a year, and every time Heracles came close to capturing her, she slipped from his grasp.

Until the day when Heracles saw the hind drink from the river bank. She lapped up the cool water and was not paying attention.

Heracles scooped her up but injured the hind in the process. This was the only way she would not run off.

Having accomplished this third task, Heracles returned to Erymanthus with the hind in his arms.

Fourth Labor

The fourth test on Heracles's great quest was to capture the Erymanthian boar and bring him back to the king.

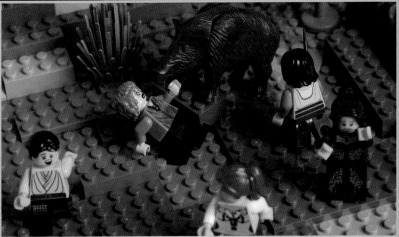

The boar roamed the great Erymanthus mountains and would attack travelers and other animals.

While Heracles ventured off to defeat the boar, he visited his friend Pholus, who was a centaur.

Pholus and Heracles dined together, but Heracles got thirsty and asked for wine. The only wine that Pholus had to offer was a bottle that was meant to be shared amongst the centaurs only.

Heracles insisted, urging Pholus to break his promise so they could drink the wine together.

In the end, he relented, and Pholus and Heracles drank up the wine.

This was a big mistake, because the god Dionysus had given the sacred wine to the centaurs and told them not to drink it for four generations.

The other centaurs discovered what had transpired and became enraged. They armed themselves with boulders and heavy fir branches.

Heracles fended them off, shooting arrows at the group of centaurs.

Heracles struck Chiron, not realizing that the two had been childhood friends.

Chiron was doomed to suffer, for the arrowhead had been soaked in the poisoned blood of the Hydra.

Pholus came along and saw what had happened. He removed the poisoned arrow and examined it, marveling at how the tiny arrowhead could kill such a great and strong centaur.

He lost his grip and dropped the arrow, which pierced his foot.

Pholus died instantly.

Heracles left the centaurs' home and continued to look for the boar. He tracked it all across the mountainside.

He found the boar on a snowy peak and cornered him. He shot the boar with an arrow to slow him down.

And Heracles was able to tie up and capture the great beast.

Heracles returned to Mycenae with the wild boar and presented it to the king.

Fifth Labor

Eurystheus decreed that Heracles's fifth labor must be to clean out the Augean stables. This infuriated Heracles, as he thought very highly of himself and did not want to be doing filthy labor.

The Augean stables were massive, holding thousands of animals of all kinds. The stables had been there for many generations, so the task of cleaning them out was quite daunting.

Heracles approached Augeas and offered to clean the stables but did not tell him that he had been ordered to do so by Eurystheus.

Heracles built a vast trench alongside the stables and filled it with water.

Augeas was delighted and promised to give Heracles a tenth of his cattle if he finished the job.

The trench carried away all of the filth from the stable stalls, and ensured that the stables would continue to stay clean.

After he finished, Augeas discovered that Heracles had lied to him and refused to give him the reward.

They went to court to determine whether or not Augeas owed Heracles the livestock for doing the work in the stables.

Augeas's son testified against him, telling the truth that Augeas had made the promise to Heracles.

Augeas flew into a rage and banished his son and Heracles before the verdict could be delivered.

Heracles returned to Mycenae, and Eurystheus declared that Heracles had behaved ignobly and the labor did not count.

Sixth Labor

Setting back out on his quest, Heracles was tasked to kill the Stymphalian birds.

These were massive, man-eating birds that had sharp bronze beaks and slashing metallic feathers that could be used as weapons. They were owned by Ares, the god of war.

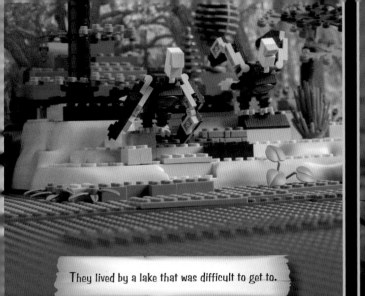

They lived by a lake that was difficult to get to.

Heracles was intimidated and didn't know how to gain an advantage over the birds.

Athena noticed the difficulty that Heracles was having and decided to help him. She gave him a large bronze rattle that had been forged by Hephaestus, the smith god.

Heracles took the rattle nearer to the birds and began to vigorously shake it.

The birds became scared by the unknown noise and flew from the safety of their trees.

Heracles took advantage of his opportunity and drew out his bow.

Heracles aimed his poisoned arrows at the great flying beasts . . .

One by one . . .

and tore them from the sky.

Victoriously, he killed them all. He was now halfway through his labors.

Seventh Labor

Heracles was then sent to capture the Cretan bull. This was not very difficult, as King Minos already had the bull. He offered the bull to Heracles.

Because of his pride, Heracles refused the help and wanted to conquer the bull on his own.

He came upon the bull and prepared to lasso the creature.

The Cretan bull was now his prisoner.

Heracles brought him back to King Eurystheus, who wanted to sacrifice the bull to Hera.

Hera refused because she did not want to honor Heracles, so they let the bull free and it continued on its rampage toward the city of Marathon.

Eighth Labor

The next task was to capture the mares of Diomedes, who was a strong and powerful giant and the King of Thrace.

The mares were beautiful and wild, but they had a flaw. They devoured human flesh.

Upon his arrival, Heracles immediately overpowered Diomedes and chained him.

He went to the stables where the mares lived and beat away the guards.

He gave the mares a snack, and Diomedes was no longer.

The remaining soldiers under Diomedes fought back, trying to regain control of the stables.

Heracles told his friend Abderos, who was the son of Hermes, to look after the mares while he fought the soldiers.

Heracles went off to fight the soldiers, defeating them one by one.

Meanwhile, the mares got hungry and ate Abderos.

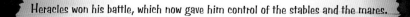
Heracles won his battle, which now gave him control of the stables and the mares.

He returned to check on Abderos and found his friend dead.

Forlorn about the loss of his friend, but victorious nonetheless, Heracles brought the mares of Diomedes back with him to Mycenae.

Eurystheus dedicated the horses to Hera, who looked after them and their offspring.

Ninth Labor

Heracles's next task was to obtain the girdle of Hippolyte on behalf of Eurystheus's daughter, Admeta.

Hippolyte was queen of the Amazons, a tribe of fierce and beautiful warrior women. These women only raised their female children, and no men were allowed in their society.

The girdle symbolized Hippolyte's status as queen and premier warrior and was a special gift from her father, Ares, the god of war.

When they arrived, Hippolyte offered to give Heracles the girdle as a gift,

Heracles formed a band of men together to assist him with his task. They traveled across the Black Sea to reach the Amazonian women.

because even though she was a great fighter, she was also kind and diplomatic.

Hera witnessed this easy transaction and became upset. She greatly wished for Heracles's downfall, so she disguised herself as one of the Amazon women and spread rumors that Heracles was plotting to abduct their queen.

The fierce Amazon women collected their weapons and went to face Heracles.

They attacked, and so began a devastating and bloody battle.

But Heracles managed to kill even the most ferocious of fighters.

He captured the strongest of the fighters, a warrior named Melanippe, and brought her to Hippolyte.

Hippolyte reluctantly surrendered her girdle to Heracles, thus ending the battle and the ninth labor.

Tenth Labor

After bringing Hippolyte's girdle to Eurystheus, Heracles was sent to fetch the Cattle of Geryon. Geryon was a beastly giant who lived on the island of Erytheia.

The island was protected by Geryon's brother, Orthus, and his ferocious dog.

Along his journey to Erytheia, Heracles came across many ferocious animals that threatened to slow him down. But Heracles was strong and swift, and he was able to continue on his trek.

He passed through a beautiful valley and stopped to build the city of Hecatompylos.

He encountered the giant rock mountain where Perseus had turned Atlas to stone. Because it was in his way, Heracles smashed clear through the mountain, creating the rock of Gibraltar and one of the North African peaks.

Water from the sea flowed through it, connecting both the Mediterranean Sea and the Atlantic Ocean.

Heracles arrived at the island of Erytheia, and right away encountered Orthus's vicious dog.

Taking his mighty club, Heracles crushed the dog.

Orthus saw what happened and attacked Heracles. Swift with his heavy weapon, Heracles repeated his blows and killed Orthus.

Heracles was now free to steal the horses, but Geryon saw him.

Geryon was much stronger than his brother and a trying battle ensued.

Eventually, Heracles broke out his bow and arrows and shot Geryon, killing the giant.

But the struggle was not over. As Heracles was leaving with the prized animals, two sons of Poseidon blocked his way.

Heracles killed them both.

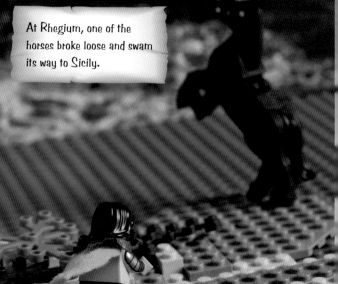

At Rhegium, one of the horses broke loose and swam its way to Sicily.

Another of Poseidon's sons, Eryx, found the horse and kept it as his own.

Heracles discovered the animal and that Eryx had taken him. Eryx told Heracles that if he could beat him in a wrestling match, then he could keep the animal.

Heracles agreed and quickly defeated Eryx.

Victorious, he returned to Mycenae with all of the animals, which were promptly slaughtered by Hera in sacrifice.

Eleventh Labor

Feeling as if Heracles had cheated his way through the Hydra and the Augean stables, Eurystheus decided to add an additional two tasks. The eleventh labor was to steal Zeus's golden apples, which had been a wedding present from Gaia, the mother of the earth.

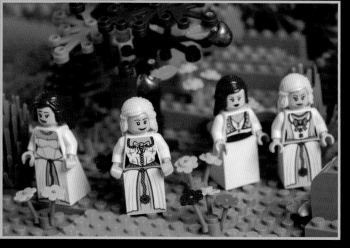

The apples were guarded by four nymphs, called the Hesperides. They were the daughters of Atlas, the Titan who held up the sky.

The apples were so precious that they were also protected by Ladon, a giant and ferocious dragon.

Heracles was unsure where to find the Garden of Hesperides, so he wandered around the deserts and vast lands of Africa, Arabia, and parts of Asia, which were often treacherous.

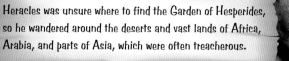

Heracles traveled through Thessaly, coming across an evil giant named Termerus.

Termerus would smash his forehead against the heads of other travelers, taking great delight in killing them.

When the giant attempted to serve the same fate to Heracles, he met an ugly end.

Termerus shattered into pieces as soon as his skull collided with Heracles's strong brow.

Heracles continued his trek, making his way to the river Echedorus. There he met Cycnus, a malevolent son of Ares.

Heracles kindly asked Cycnus how to get to the garden, but the cruel man refused and challenged him to a fight.

Naturally, Heracles swiftly killed him.

Ares was so upset by his son's demise that he appeared to Heracles to fight him himself.

Zeus intervened, because as the father of both Ares and Heracles, he did not want either to perish. He flashed a lightning bolt between the dueling men and separated them.

Moving on, Heracles traveled through Illyria and met lovely nymphs, who were also the daughters of Zeus.

They told him that the man he needed to see was Nereus, an old river god and a seer. The nymphs instructed Heracles to bind the god while he slept.

Heracles did exactly as they said, and Nereus told him where to go.

Along the way, Heracles passed Prometheus, who was chained to a rock. Every day, a bird would come and eat his liver as punishment for giving fire to mankind.

Heracles killed the bird that pecked away at Prometheus.

He unchained him, and Prometheus was forever grateful. He warned Heracles that stealing Zeus's apples was very dangerous, for the wrath of Zeus was great.

Heracles came upon Atlas, who was holding up the sky.

He told Heracles that he was better off asking Atlas to do the job for him.

He asked the great Titan if he could steal the golden apples for him, and in return he would hold up the sky for him for a little while.

Atlas agreed and went off to the garden.

When he arrived, he put the dragon to sleep by playing music for him.

While the dragon slept, Atlas killed him.

Atlas arrived at the tree and outwitted the nymphs who guarded it.

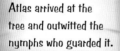

He stole the golden apples and returned to where Heracles waited.

Atlas realized how much he enjoyed not bearing the weight of the world on his shoulders, and he told Heracles that he planned to leave him there.

But Heracles was very cunning. He slyly asked Atlas to hold the sky up for a minute while Heracles better adjusted himself to hold the sky. Atlas complied, and Heracles ran away with the apples.

Heracles returned to give the golden apples to Eurystheus.

Athena returned the apples to the Garden of Hesperides, knowing that was where they truly belonged.

Eurystheus was angry that Heracles had been so successful in his tasks, so he plotted to give him one that would be utterly impossible.

Twelfth Labor

Eurystheus issued the final, most difficult labor for Heracles's punishment for killing his own children. He instructed Heracles to go to the depths of the Underworld, where no mortals could leave, and capture Cerberus, the vicious, three-headed hellhound.

The trip was so daunting, that Heracles journeyed to Eleusis to seek the guidance of Eumpolpuc and be initiated in the Eleusinian Mysteries. This would teach Heracles how to go down to the Underworld and return alive.

The priest proclaimed the sacred religious rites, providing good luck to Heracles.

Heracles traveled Taenarum, a city where there was a gateway to the Underworld.

Entering the gates, he journeyed to the depths below, preparing for the tests that would meet him along the way.

He first encountered a terrifying ghost.

Heracles's initial instinct was to fight the ghost, but Hermes intervened and explained that he was just a fantasma—a figment that could not harm Heracles.

Next he was confronted by Menoetius, a Titan god of violence and anger who had been banished forever to the Underworld by Zeus.

Seeing the fight, Persephone arrived and broke the two men apart.

Heracles finally reached the main gates to the Underworld, where Hades stood blocking his path.

Heracles shot the god with an arrow and told him that he planned to capture Cerberus.

Unfazed, Hades deflected the arrow and told Heracles that he could take the great hellhound on one condition: he do it with only his bare hands.

Heracles agreed to the terms and attacked the dog.

During the heated battle, Heracles dodged the snapping teeth and slashing tail of the vicious animal. He grasped all three heads at the same time

and wrestled the dog to the ground.

Heracles placed the dog in shackles and brought him to Eurystheus, who was utterly horrified and dismayed.

Eurystheus was forced to accept that Heracles had successfully completed his labors and could be set free.

Heracles returned Cerberus to its rightful place in the Underworld.

Heracles and Admetus

In the city of Pherae in Thessaly, there once lived a kind and well-loved king named Admetus.

Long ago, when Apollo fled Olympus, King Admetus had welcomed him to Pherae with open arms.

When Zeus returned Apollo to his position, he remembered Admetus's kindness, and Admetus became the king's patron, bestowing blessings and favors upon him.

One day King Admetus became very ill. As he lay on his deathbed, Apollo came to him and told him of a way he could escape death. He would need a mortal to offer to die on his behalf.

His subjects were heartbroken to see their beloved king die, but no one, not even the king's elderly parents, would volunteer to die in his place.

Then Alcestis, his wife and the loving mother to his children, stepped forward. She offered to sacrifice herself so that her husband could live.

Thanatos, god of death, came to claim her.

Alcestis prepared for her end, bidding her children and her husband a teary, sad farewell. She told her husband to remember her sacrifice and had him promise her that he would not marry again.

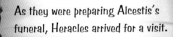

As they were preparing Alcestis's funeral, Heracles arrived for a visit.

He was taken to see the king, who, despite his sorrow, welcomed the hero warmly.

Heracles noticed that the king was dressed in robes of mourning. He inquired who had died. Admetus wished not to upset his guest, or give him cause to leave, so he told Heracles that it had been some distant relative.

A servant arrived to take Heracles to his room, and he followed her cheerfully.

He noticed the servant was upset, and inquired why she would be so moved by the death of someone unknown to her.

The servant began to cry, and she was so upset that she couldn't help but tell Heracles the whole story. It was no unknown woman, but the queen who had died.

Heracles felt guilty for being so cheerful and for interrupting this sad scene. He wished to show his gratitude to his host for being so welcoming despite his own troubles. He determined to find a way to save Alcestis.

So Heracles made his way to Alcestis's grave to wait for Thanatos to bring her to Hades.

When the god of death arrived, Heracles ambushed him.

He captured Thanatos and held him until the god agreed to let Alcestis live.

Heracles brought Alcestis to King Admetus, disguising her under a hood.

He apologized to Admetus for imposing on his hospitality during a time of such grief. He offered him the veiled woman to be his handmaid, as a sign of his gratitude.

Admetus told Heracles he had concealed his grief so as not to share it with his guest or make him feel unwelcome.

He said that while he thanked Heracles for his gift, he had nowhere for the woman to stay: he could not have her stay with him or go to his wife's quarters.

Heracles hid his true thoughts on the matter and told Admetus that he wished he could save the king's wife to repay his kindness.

He convinced King Admetus to accept his gift and take the woman to the house.

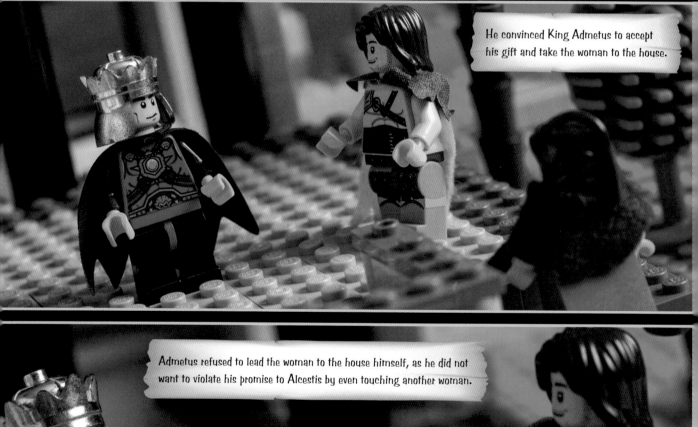

Admetus refused to lead the woman to the house himself, as he did not want to violate his promise to Alcestis by even touching another woman.

Heracles was adamant, and so King Admetus reluctantly took her by the hand.

As he did so, Heracles pulled the hood from Alcestis's face, revealing the king's wife alive and well.

Admetus was overjoyed and thanked Heracles for this miracle.

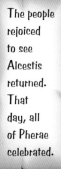

The people rejoiced to see Alcestis returned. That day, all of Pherae celebrated.

Heracles and Eurytus

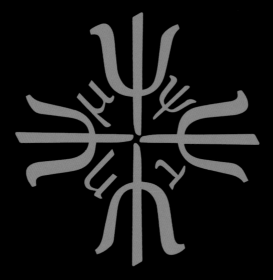

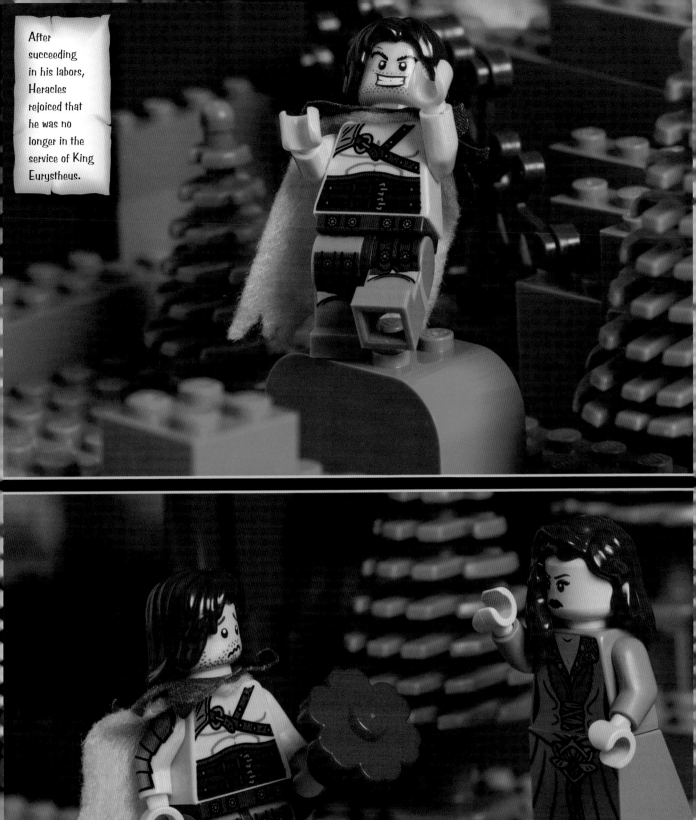

After succeeding in his labors, Heracles rejoiced that he was no longer in the service of King Eurystheus.

Having killed all of their children, it was no longer an option to remain married to Megara.

So Heracles sought off to find a new match. He quickly became interested in the lovely Iole. She was the daughter of Eurytus, the king of Oechalia who had helped teach Heracles archery as a young boy.

King Eurytus decreed that if a suitor wanted to win the hand of Iole in marriage, then he would have to defeat Eurytus and his brawny sons in an archery contest.

Heracles headed to Oechalia to take up the challenge.

As the grandson of Apollo, the god of archery, the skilled Eurytus and his sons all presented great competition for Heracles.

But their skill and aim were not quite great enough.

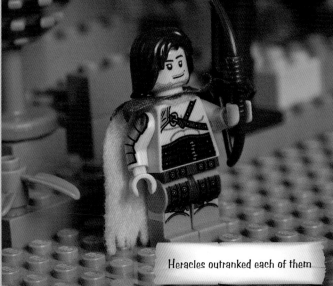

Heracles outranked each of them

with perfect bull's-eyes.

Eurytus knew the story of what Heracles had done to Megara's children and worried deeply about allowing Heracles to wed Iole.

His son Iphitus had become very friendly with Heracles through the archery contest and did his best to convince his father that he would be a good match for Iole.

Eurytus argued back, deciding once and for all that Heracles would not be allowed to marry his daughter, despite having proven that he was a superior bowman.

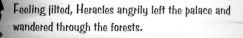

Feeling jilted, Heracles angrily left the palace and wandered through the forests.

While he was gone, thieves stole mares from the royal herd.

Eurytus pointed the finger at Heracles, imagining that he had stolen the herd out of revenge.

Iphitus once again came to Heracles's defense, telling his father that he would go find Heracles and that the two would seek out the stolen mares themselves.

Iphitus found Heracles in the forest and explained what had happened.

They searched far and wide for the missing herd, hoping to return them to Eurytus and clear Heracles's name. Despite their efforts, the mares were nowhere to be found.

They searched along a high cliff, where Hera looked on loathingly. She struck Heracles with powerful sorcery, sending him into a fit of madness.

Taken over by the madness that Hera had inflicted upon him, Heracles lifted Iphitus into the air and tossed him off the cliff.

In a frenzy, Heracles approached his friend, who stood at the edge of the rocky cliff overlooking the lands below.

Heracles and Omphale

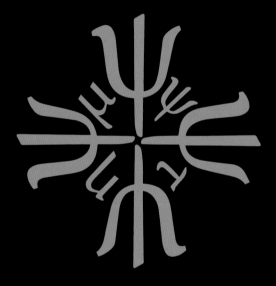

When Heracles saw what he had done to his friend Iphitus in his madness, he was filled with guilt and sorrow.

He wandered across the earth seeking a priest-king who could purify him, but none would help him.

He finally met Deiphobus, who was able to purify him.

Despite this, the gods still punished him, cursing him with a terrible illness, which was something the strong and healthy hero had never experienced before.

The gods came to him and told him that his affliction would be ended if he were sold into slavery for three years.

Heracles was sent to Asia and sold to a woman named Omphale, who was the daughter of Iardanus and the queen of the country Maeonia.

As soon as the money for his sale reached the hands of Iphitus's family, Heracles's illness disappeared.

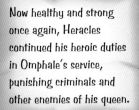

Now healthy and strong once again, Heracles continued his heroic duties in Omphale's service, punishing criminals and other enemies of his queen.

Omphale was impressed with his good work, and when she discovered that he was the son of Zeus, she raised him to his proper standing and married him.

Heracles forgot his duties as a hero and became indulgent and pampered.

Meanwhile Omphale shamed him by dressing in his lion skin and carrying around his club.

Sometimes she would dress him in women's clothing.

But Heracles's passion for the beautiful woman kept him content and docile, and he spent much of his time chatting with the servant girls over his sewing.

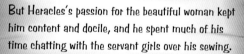

When Heracles's three years of servitude were up, he suddenly came to his senses and was angry that he had neglected his righteous quest. He took his lion skin from Omphale and left her, resolving to take revenge on his enemies.

Heracles and Deianira

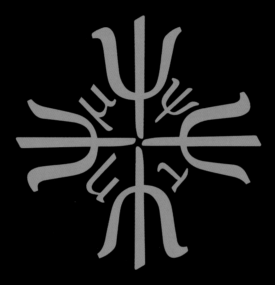

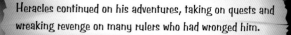

Heracles continued on his adventures, taking on quests and wreaking revenge on many rulers who had wronged him.

In his travels, he heard news of a beautiful woman named Deianira, who was the daughter of King Oeneus.

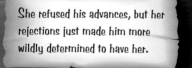

Deianira was so beautiful that she was constantly visited by suitors seeking her hand. She hated it.

Her most persistent and obnoxious suitor was the river god Achelous, who came to her disguised in many different forms.

She refused his advances, but her rejections just made him more wildly determined to have her.

King Oeneus wished for Deianira to accept Achelous, since he was such an old and powerful god.

But just then Heracles arrived in the throne room, armed and ready for battle. Achelous was furious to see him.

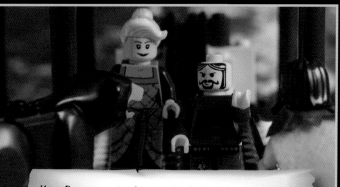

King Oeneus, seeing his opportunity to gain one powerful son-in-law or another, told the suitors that he would wed his daughter to whichever of them beat the other in combat.

They met for their battle, Heracles armed with his bow.

As the hero prepared to let fly his arrows, the river god transformed himself into a gigantic bull.

The fight became a wrestling contest, and strong Heracles had the upper hand.

The tricky god tried to throw Heracles from him by changing into a snake, but Heracles avoided his fangs.

Then Achelous became a great bull again, and they continued to fight. Heracles reached down and grasped one of the bull's horns, and pulled with all his might, tearing the horn off Achelous's head.

Seeing he had been soundly defeated, the river god gave up. He gave Heracles the Horn of Plenty in exchange for his own horn.

Heracles and Deianira were married and lived happily. Deianira soon bore her husband a son named Hyllus.

Then Heracles continued out on his adventures, bringing Hyllus and Deianira along.

Heracles and Nessus

Along their journey, Heracles, Deianira, and Hyllus came to a rushing river. The centaur Nessus was a ferryman of the river Euenos and offered to carry them across.

Heracles needed no assistance and carried the young Hyllus across the river to safety.

Deianira accepted Nessus's offer to escort her across the river, for the water was treacherous.

While Nessus carried Deianira across the river, he became infatuated with the beautiful woman.

Against her will, Nessus tried to embrace Deianira.

Deianira shrieked, crying out to her husband for help.

From the riverbank, Heracles and Hyllus saw her struggling. Heracles pulled out one of the venomous arrows from the Hydra . . .

. . . and shot Nessus clear through the heart.

The lecherous centaur came upon the shore, slowly fading from the arrow wound.

Unbeknownst to Heracles, Nessus reached out for Deianira and told her that his blood had special properties. He said that if she were to save some of his blood and soak Heracles's clothing in it, her husband would never be unfaithful.

Foolishly, Deianira believed him and collected the blood of the centaur in a vial just before he died.

Heracles, Iole, and Deianira

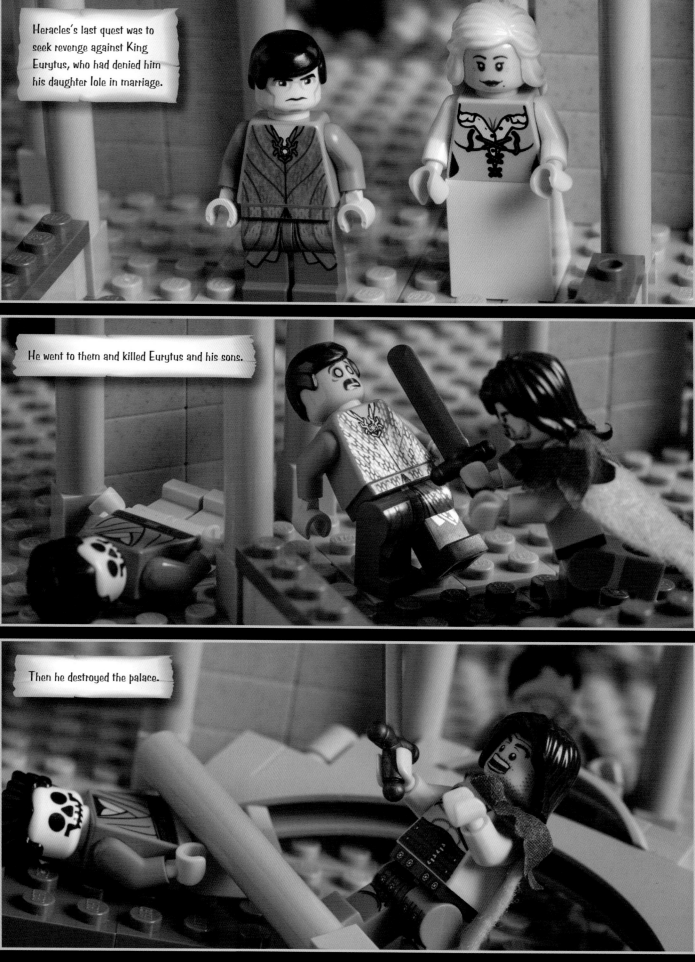

Heracles's last quest was to seek revenge against King Eurytus, who had denied him his daughter Iole in marriage.

He went to them and killed Eurytus and his sons.

Then he destroyed the palace.

When the battle was done, Heracles's messenger Lichas brought the prisoners to Deianira and told her they were at her mercy. Among the prisoners was Iole.

Deianira was kind and took pity on the prisoners, including the beautiful Iole. She recognized that the girl was clearly noble born and asked her who she was.

But the girl would not tell her.

Still, Deianira treated her and the other prisoners with great care and kindness.

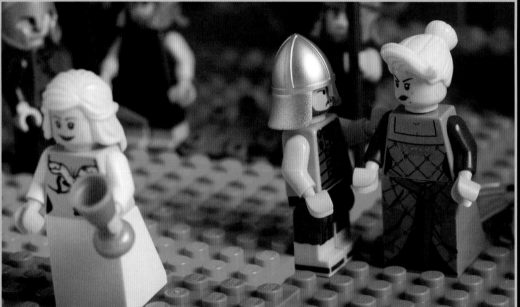

Another messenger came and told Deianira who the woman was. She was Iole, who Heracles once loved, and it was for her that they came to this place and destroyed the palace. Deianira was very upset, but she did not take her anger out on Iole, since she had done Deianira no wrong.

Still, she was heartbroken at the thought of losing Heracles, so she decided to use the centaur blood she had gotten from Nessus so that he would love no one else.

She took a piece of wool and secretly dyed it red with the blood of the centaur.

Then she made it into a beautiful red tunic for Heracles to wear at an upcoming ceremony where he would give offerings to the gods.

She gave the tunic to a messenger named Lichas and sent him to deliver it to Heracles as a gift from her.

She instructed him that no one was to wear it but Heracles, and that he should not wear it in sunlight until the day of the offering when he would present himself to the gods.

Several days passed and Deianira had no news of Heracles, so she sent their son Hyllus to tell him that she was worried and to ask him to return to her.

When he had gone, Deianira went back to the room where she had secretly dyed the tunic. The wool she had discarded lay by the window, and she saw that where the sun had touched it, the fabric had crumbled and was oozing poisonous foam.

Hyllus returned to Deianira in a fury, yelling that he wished she were not his mother.

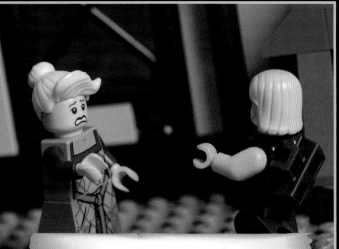

Deianira asked him what he meant, and Hyllus mournfully cried that she had deprived him of his father.

Then he explained what had happened.

When Heracles received the tunic from Lichas, he was very pleased with the gift. He put it on the morning of the offering.

Wearing the lovely tunic, he stepped forward to begin the ceremony.

He stepped close to the flame for the offering, and the fire rose suddenly.

Heracles began to sweat, and the tunic stuck to his body as if it were welded to him.

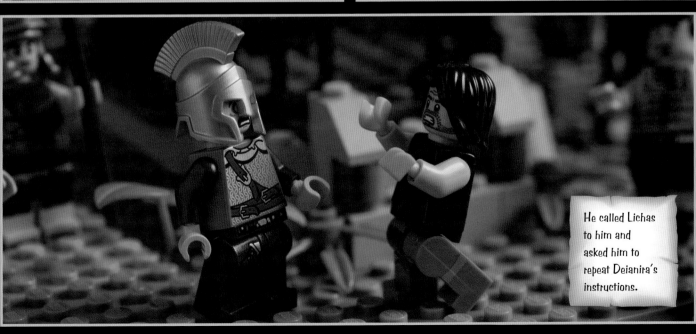

He called Lichas to him and asked him to repeat Deianira's instructions.

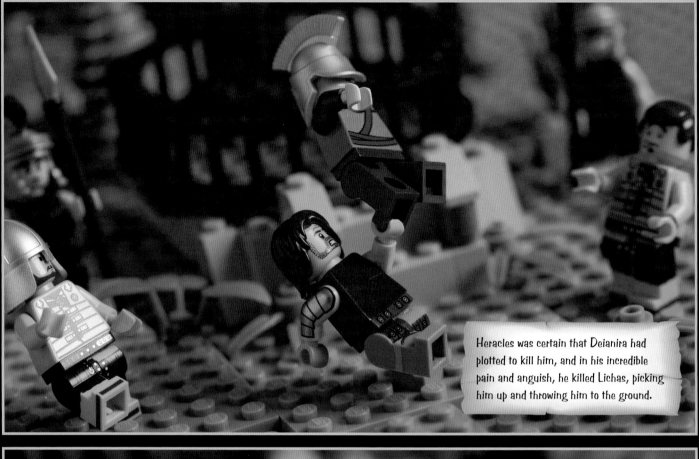

Heracles was certain that Deianira had plotted to kill him, and in his incredible pain and anguish, he killed Lichas, picking him up and throwing him to the ground.

He screamed out in agony and anger, cursing his marriage and his wife as the tunic continued to weep poison onto his skin. Heracles knew that he was going to die.

He asked Hyllus to help him to a ship, so that he could die in his own lands. Hyllus returned to prepare the ship.

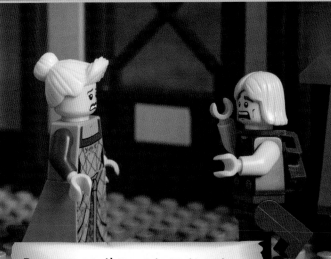

Finishing his tale, Hyllus cried out to his mother, "You have killed the most glorious hero of all time!"

Deianira did not answer him but turned and left the room in silence.

There was a servant who had overheard the whole affair, and she went to Hyllus after his mother had left. She told the boy that he had been unjust to his mother and explained how the wicked centaur had tricked her.

Hyllus regretted his harsh words and sought out his mother to apologize. But it was too late: she had put a sword through her chest and was dead.

Heracles soon arrived, and begged Hyllus to kill him so that he would not be slain by his wife's hand.

Hyllus explained that Deianira had meant no harm and told his father how she had been tricked by the centaur. Heracles's anger became sorrow as Hyllus told him what had happened and how Deianira had killed herself.

Heracles then had his son betrothed to the beautiful Iole.

But Heracles was still dying. An oracle came to him and told him that he would die on Mount Oeta, so he set off for the peak.

He had his friends help him build a great funeral pyre right at the top of the mountain.

Then he climbed onto the pyre.

A bolt of lightning struck the wooden structure and set it ablaze!

A cloud floated from the heavens and surrounded the pyre. The cloud took Heracles and brought him up to Olympus. When the fire had finished burning, his friends searched the ashes, but his bones were nowhere to be found.

When Heracles arrived in Olympus, the other gods welcomed him as a hero and gave him the gift of immortality. They also allowed him a place in the circle of the gods.

Hera reconciled with him, putting an end to their bitter conflict.

As a sign of her goodwill, she allowed Heracles to take her daughter Hebe, the goddess of everlasting life, as his Olympian wife. Thus ended the adventures of the great hero Heracles.

Jason and the Golden Fleece

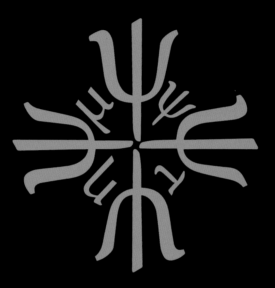

Once there was a country called Iolcus, ruled by a king named Aeson and his queen Alcimede. They had a young son named Jason who was to inherit his father's throne.

Aeson's stepbrother, Pelias, had a thirst for power and wanted the throne for himself.

So he challenged King Aeson to a fight. Pelias beat his brother soundly.

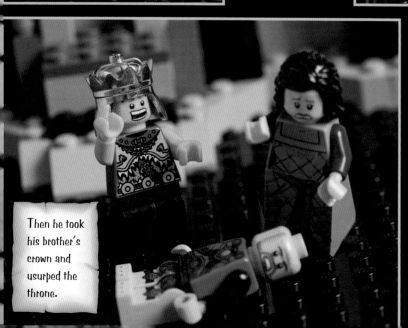

Then he took his brother's crown and usurped the throne.

To prevent any challengers from threatening his rule, Pelias had Aeson thrown in prison and ordered much of his family to be killed.

Obsessed with retaining his ill-gotten throne, Pelias consulted an oracle. The seer told him that a man with one sandal would finish him.

Meanwhile, Alcimede was able to escape Pelias's wrath, fleeing into the wilderness with her child clutched tightly in her arms.

In the woods she met the wise centaur Chiron. Alcimede was very concerned for the safety of her child, but Chiron promised to keep Jason safe. With many tears, Alcimede gave her child over to the centaur to raise the boy and be his mentor.

True to his word, Chiron kept the boy safe from Pelias and taught him many skills with weapons and battle tactics.

Under Chiron's care and instruction, Jason grew into a smart and strong young man. The centaur taught him all that he needed to know to be a great warrior. So once he was old enough, Jason decided to return to his home in Iolcus.

Jason set out for Iolcus, but he had not gone far before he came to a strong and perilous river.

Looking along the river bank, he saw an old woman nearby who was trying to cross the river. He gallantly offered to help her across.

He put the old woman onto his back and began to make his way across the rushing river.

As he went, the current pulled at one of his sandals, sweeping it off his foot and sending it floating away from him on the swiftly moving water.

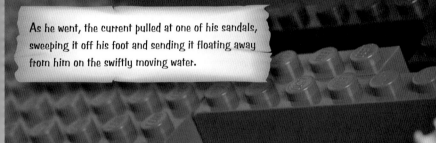

They arrived at the other side of the river safely, and Jason helped the woman off his back. When he turned to look at her, she had transformed, and now looked young and radiantly beautiful. She was the goddess Hera.

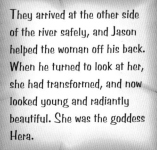

Hera told Jason that she hated Pelias, because he paid tribute and worshipped all of the gods except for her. But Hera was pleased with Jason for helping her, so from this point on, he would travel with her blessing.

After continuing on his journey, Jason soon arrived at the gates of Iolcus.

Seeing that he wore only one sandal, the man at the gate ran to tell Pelias that a stranger with one sandal had arrived.

Jason went to the throne room to meet with Pelias and demanded that the false king give him back the kingdom that was rightfully his.

Wicked Pelias told Jason he could have his kingdom if he brought him the Golden Fleece of a magical ram owned by Zeus. Pelias thought that this would be a good way to get rid of the young man, since he believed the task was impossible.

Jason gathered a crew of strong, brave men to join him on his quest.

The great hero Heracles himself even joined them on the journey.

Together they boarded a ship, called the *Argo*, and set out on their journey. The group of men would come to be called the Argonauts.

Their first stop was on an island called Lemnos, which was inhabited only by women. These women had neglected their prayers to Aphrodite, and as punishment the goddess cursed them, making them smell foul and making their faces ugly until their husbands did not want to look on them. Furious at the rejection, the women killed their husbands while they slept, and from then on there had been no men on the island. The Argonauts did not visit long.

Next they sailed the *Argo* to Samothrace, where an ancient group of gods called the Kabeiroi greeted them warmly and offered them food and hospitality. They rested and celebrated before moving on with their journey.

Phineas was plagued by vicious harpies, who would steal or destroy any food the old man had.

Their next stop was on the island of Thrace, where they found a blind prophet named Phineas imprisoned.

The Argonauts took up arms against the monsters and battled them.

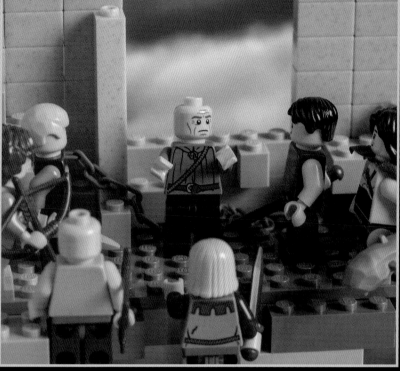

slaying them both and rescuing the seer.

Phineas was grateful to the men for freeing him. In return for his rescue, he told the Argonauts where to find the Golden Fleece. The fleece is to be found in Colchis, but to get there they must pass through the treacherous Symplegades, or "clashing rocks," that guarded the entrance to the Black Sea.

Phineas then prophesied that Jason would be the first man to successfully navigate through the Symplegades.

Armed with new information, the men returned to the *Argo* and set sail.

True to Phineas's prediction, Jason made his way through the Symplegades safely.

When they reached Colchis, Jason went to see the ruler, who was called King Aietes. Jason asked him directly if he would give him the Golden Fleece.

King Aietes agreed to give him the fleece as soon as Jason performed several superhuman tasks for him.

Aietes's daughter, Medea, had watched with interest as Jason spoke with her father. She came to him and offered to help him with the challenges her father had planned, but in return, she wanted Jason to marry her. He agreed.

Jason's first task was to feed a fire-breathing bull. Medea accompanied him, and together they finished the job quickly.

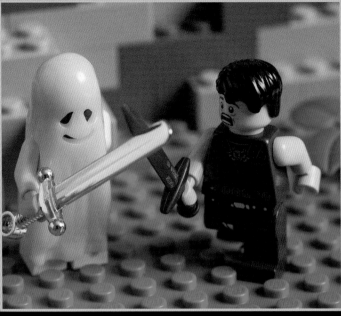

Next he was ordered to plow a field and plant dragon's teeth. Medea joined him and warned him that when planted, the teeth would grow into dangerous phantom warriors.

Thanks to Medea's warning, Jason was not caught unawares, and he defeated the warriors swiftly.

Back at the castle, Aietes spoke to his daughter and told her about his final plan to get rid of Jason. He would hold a great feast in the young man's honor, and when he was distracted, kill him.

Medea betrayed her father. She went to Jason to warn him of Aietes's plan.

She then told Jason where he could find the Golden Fleece: nailed to a tree and guarded by a vicious monster. Together, they went to fetch the prize.

Medea used her skill in witchcraft to create a sleeping potion and used it to put the creature guarding the fleece to sleep.

While it dozed, Jason walked past and took the Golden Fleece from the tree. Then, with the fleece in hand, Jason, Medea, and the Argonauts returned to the ship and departed before King Aietes could stop them.

Their return journey did not go smoothly, and the *Argo* was caught in a terrible storm. The sea surged and the wind howled as the storm threatened to tear the ship to pieces. The crew was sure they would die, and they began to pray to Apollo to protect them.

As the next crack of lightning lit the sky, the crew saw that they had come to an island.

They landed and there found a powerful nymph who helped to quell the storm, allowing them to continue safely on their way home.

At long last they arrived back at the docks of Iolcus, rejoicing to have finished their quest safely and successfully.

But Iolcus had not been peaceful in their absence: Jason learned that King Pelias had killed his father.

Alcimede, his mother, had died of heartbreak at the loss of her husband.

He presented the Golden Fleece to the king, but it was no use.

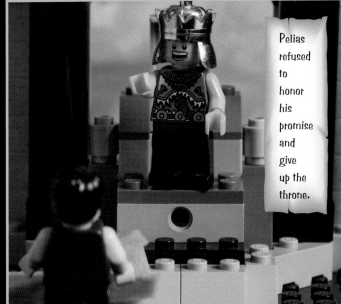

Pelias refused to honor his promise and give up the throne.

So Medea used her witchcraft, casting a spell to put Pelias into a very deep sleep.

When his daughters came to see him, Medea told them that he had died and that the only way to bring him back to life was to boil him.

They followed her instructions and put him into the royal bath.

They filled the bath with boiling water, killing the cruel king once and for all.

Jason and Medea lived happily for some time, exchanging their life of adventure for a more domestic existence. They married and had several children.

But one day the powerful king of Corinth offered to Jason the king's own daughter in marriage.

Jason accepted and sent Medea away from him. She was filled with a terrible murderous rage.

In revenge, she killed Jason's betrothed, then slaughtered her and Jason's children in cold blood.

Jason was destroyed by grief, and he became a wanderer, walking aimlessly across the earth.

In his travels he came upon a beached ship
and realized it was the *Argo*. He sat under
its mast to think a while and fell asleep.

As he was
sleeping, a
great beam
fell from
the upper
parts of the
decaying
ship and
landed
on Jason,
killing him.

About the Authors

Amanda Brack is a freelance illustrator who loves dogs of all shapes and sizes, old horror movies, and homemade smoothies. She spent most of her childhood with her brothers constructing expansive Lego towns and fighting over the best bricks. She graduated from the School of the Museum of Fine Arts and is currently living near Boston, Massachusetts.

Monica Sweeney works in publishing and is also pursuing her master's degree. She enjoys reading anything from Middle English to graphic novels, restaurant-hopping, old movie theaters, and Cape Cod beaches. She is writing partners with Becky Thomas and is the coauthor of *Brick Shakespeare: The Tragedies*, *Brick Shakespeare: The Comedies*, and *Brick Fairytales*. Monica lives in Boston, Massachusetts.

Becky Thomas is a nerdy lady who enjoys reading, writing, and playing board games. She loves Jane Austen and superhero comic books. She is the coauthor, with John McCann and Monica Sweeney, of *Brick Shakespeare: The Tragedies*, *Brick Shakespeare: The Comedies*, and *Brick Fairytales*. She lives with her husband, Patrick, and their cats, Leo and Leia, in Burlington, Massachusetts.

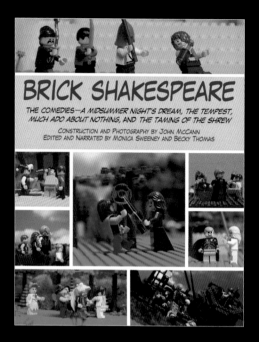

Brick Shakespeare

The Comedies—*A Midsummer Night's Dream, The Tempest, Much Ado About Nothing*, and *The Taming of the Shrew*

Construction and Photography by John McCann

Edited and Narrated by Monica Sweeney and Becky Thomas

Explore four of Shakespeare's comedies like never before—with LEGO bricks! This book presents Shakespeare's most delightful comedies, *A Midsummer Night's Dream, Much Ado About Nothing, The Taming of the Shrew,* and *The Tempest,* in one thousand amazing color photographs. This unique adaptation of the world's most famous plays stays true to Shakespeare's original text, while giving audiences an exciting new perspective as the stories are retold with the universally beloved construction toy.

Get caught up in hilarious misadventures as brick Puck leads the lovers astray through the brick forests of Athens. Watch Cupid kill with traps in the plot to marry Beatrice and Benedick. Marvel at the changing disguises of the men vying for brick Bianca's affections, and feel the churn of the ocean as Prospero sinks his brother's ship into the brick sea. These iconic stories jump off the page with fun, creative sets built brick by brick, scene by scene!

This incredible method of storytelling gives new life to Shakespeare's masterpieces. With an abridged form that maintains original Shakespearean language and modern visuals, this ode to the Bard is sure to please all audiences, from the most versed Shakespeare enthusiasts to young students and newcomers alike!

$19.95 Paperback • ISBN 978-1-62873-733-2

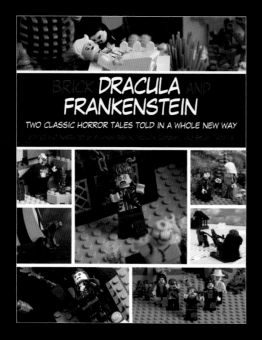

Brick Dracula and Frankenstein

Two Classic Horror Tales Told in a Whole New Way

Edited and Narrated by Amanda Brack, Monica Sweeney, and Becky Thomas

Get caught up in the two most famous scary stories of all time depicted in LEGO bricks! Creep your way through the shadowy sets of Mary Shelley's *Frankenstein* and Bram Stoker's *Dracula* in this amazing brick adaptation. With one thousand color photographs, these stories and their monsters come alive in full plastic horror!

Stare in awe as Dr. Frankenstein brings his brick monster to life in a risky science experiment, and brace yourself as the creature steps out into the world. Travel to Count Dracula's giant brick castle in Transylvania, and beware as he taunts his prey in the night. Watch brick Van Helsing discover the cause of poor Lucy's illness, and follow him as he prepares his plot to save her.

These classic horror stories are retold with a classic construction toy, staying true to their original forms in this modestly abridged collection. For young readers, LEGO adorers, and devotees to gothic literature, *Brick Dracula and Frankenstein* is a mesmerizing new take to the founding tales of fright!

$19.95 Paperback • ISBN 978-1-62914-591-1